Peaches & Cream

The Men of Haven Grove

A.D. ELLIS

Cover Photo of Caden J. by
Eric McKinney- 6:12 Photography

Quotes of Inspiration

*"If you want something long-lasting,
don't skip the friendship part."*
~We the Urban

*"I don't need anyone" is a statement often made by
those who, at some point, needed someone,
but no one showed up."*
~Sara Kuburic

Chapter 1
Hudson Riggs

THE FAMILIAR NOTIFICATION SOUND FROM ClickC*ck brought my phone to life on the bar. I picked it up and tapped out a reply as my brother, Henry, rolled his eyes.

"What?" I asked around a mouthful of burger. "I can multi-task," I said with a grin as I ate my lunch on a break from work.

Henry's bar—The Riggs Family Roadhouse—had been in our family for nearly forty years, and he did a great job running it. Good food, good beer, even better cocktails— Henry was a master mixologist—and a great, easy atmosphere. I helped a few shifts a week as I could and often found myself there on weekends as well.

Although, recently, with taking over The Juicy Peach, time hadn't been as plentiful. The family's peach orchard and general store needed some major revitalization. Little did any of us know that our uncle, Billy Riggs, had not only drunk himself to death, but he'd also nearly run the business into the ground with no hope of recovery. But the Riggs name meant something to me, and The Juicy Peach was where I'd spent my childhood and teen years, I wasn't going to let it go without a fight.

I maybe wasn't an expert, but I was smart and determined. I planned to give it a thousand percent and hope the peach orchard and little store pulled through. Both were cornerstones in the small Midwestern town of Haven Grove—as was The Roadhouse—and I wasn't going down without a fight.

"You really need some damn app to find yourself a man?" Henry asked, his usual gruff personality alive and well. He was actually one of the best people you'd ever meet—loyal, hardworking, protective, and caring, a big softie if I was being honest—but my older brother, even with his soft voice and sparkling eyes, gave off a *stay back, I'm a grump* type vibe on even the best of days.

Smirking at him, I said, "Yeah, you're doing a bang-up job without an app, huh? Got a date tonight? Last night?" I knew my brother hadn't been involved with anyone in a *very* long time. He was stand-offish and kept everything close to his chest when it came to anyone other than family.

"Me and my right hand are doing just fine, thanks," Henry groused, a flare of pink splashing his cheeks above his beard. "You really think you're going to find something serious on that thing?"

I popped an onion ring in my mouth. "Ah, see, there's the misconception." I pointed to my phone. "ClickC*ck isn't for anything serious. I don't do serious. Quick and easy is all I'm looking for."

Henry frowned. "I just don't get that. Why put time and effort into something you know is just going to end?"

Shrugging, I finished off my burger, washing it down with a long swig of water. "Rather put minimal energy into something I *know* is going to end than my whole heart into something I want to last—only to have them walk away in the end."

My brother shook his head. "They don't all leave, Hudson," he said quietly.

"*She* did," I bit out. "Look, I'm not getting into this again. She left. Period. The one guy I tried to date in high school left. Everyone leaves. So, it's easier to just do random hookups than try to date." I waved my phone as I continued. "Haven Grove isn't exactly a mecca of single, gay men, so I use this. It's not your way and I respect that. Do me the favor of doing the same."

Henry looked as if he wanted to say more, but he just grabbed a cloth and started wiping down the bar. It was an argument we had often. Our mother left when we were little. She and Dad got together very young and ended up having Henry when they were barely eighteen. My dad, Casey Joe, didn't want to get married, but Missy talked him into it—she was convincing when she set her mind to it if the stories were to be believed. Two years after Henry, I came along.

By the time she'd been a small-town mom of two boys for four years, Missy was done with it all. Done with being a mother, done with being married, done with the small town. She walked out on the three of us—not before causing some drama between Billy and Casey Joe which they never really got over—and we never heard a peep from her.

At thirty-five and thirty-three, Henry and I both still held hurt and anger, but we dealt with it differently. I was hurt and just never got serious about anyone. If I didn't want or expect them to stay, it didn't hurt when they walked away.

Henry, on the other hand, did more of a *shut himself off from everyone* type thing. After Missy left, as Henry got older, he took on the role of looking after me and our dad —not that Dad expected him to, Henry had just always been a caretaker. So, he took care of his family and kept everyone else at a distance.

As my brother and I continued chatting, I checked my ClickC*ck messages. Henry refilled my water and took away my empty plate.

"How are the trees?" he asked.

I glanced around the bar, not wanting to announce the possible demise of The Juicy Peach and the Riggs Family Orchard—both provided decent jobs in Haven Grove, and both were a huge part of the town. Seeing the place was pretty much empty, which was why I usually tried to take my lunch break later than the average Joe, I shrugged.

"From what I can gather, the bacterial spot was only on a handful of the trees. I had that guy from Georgia stop by on his way up to Wisconsin to visit his mother in the fall. He took a look at the whole farm and said it was a mild case and we'd caught it in time. Told me to use copper-based fungicide spray. Guess now, we just wait and see."

"The blooms are damn nice," Henry said, referring to

the gorgeous pale pink flowers covering the entire orchard.

"Yeah, they should start to fall pretty soon and then we'll see how the fruit comes on," I said, glancing at the incoming message on my phone.

> User54321: I'll be in the area for a bit if you're interested in meeting up.
>
> Me: Sure.

The guy only had a half-face picture for his profile—along with some shots of his abs, thighs, and back—but the little thumbnail image showed a beard, and I was an absolute slut for beards. I had to admit, the days' worth of back-and-forth messages we'd sent had me wondering about the guy. He had one of the most generic usernames possible *and* he sent fully punctuated and grammatically correct messages. Don't get me wrong, I mostly did the same, but a lot of users texted in such shorthand and acronyms it was difficult to decipher at times. The bit of silver in his beard, and the fact he didn't appear to subscribe to text-speak, made me think he was *at least* my age. Likely older.

And mmmmm, the thought of a bearded silver fox did delicious things to me.

I absolutely had every intention of meeting up with him.

We'd been texting since a few days before when his

location dinged my app and I'd found myself enjoying the bit of chatter rather than the immediate *down to fuck* and demand for me to host since they were just traveling through. I didn't mind hosting. I had a decent little place near the orchard, but some of the guys came across as damned entitled. I usually did a little digging to find out if they were in our little town with a family—wives, kids, or girlfriends were a hard no for me, I wasn't looking to ruin any families.

But this guy had been different from the start. Easy to chat with. Not demanding. Add in the beard and possible age gap, and I was sold.

"Sounds like you did the right thing with the trees," Henry was saying, pulling me from my thoughts. "How's the store?"

I ran a hand through my sandy blond hair knowing my brother would see deceit in my blue eyes if I tried to hide anything. "Let's just say, we're lucky to have that money socked away to fall back on for a while. Billy just let the whole thing go there at the end. Now that I think I have the books in order, we need to get stock built up, and do a little something creative to get people buzzing about shopping there again."

Henry shrugged. "Once you say the word, we'll talk it up in here. Half this town has always done most of their shopping at Juicy, they're not going to stop now."

"Yeah," I said, wanting to believe him. "We have location and history on our side, I just want to get everything back in tip-top shape. Right now, it's pretty embarrassing to have the locals come in for their staples.

And I'm glad we're not getting very many tourists for a while."

"You'll get 'er done, no doubt. That's why I felt best about you taking over instead of Dad."

I snorted. "Dad is in no shape to take on the orchard and store."

Casey Joe had never really been the same since Missy left us. He put on a good face, pretty much took care of us the best he could, and was known by Haven Grove as a decent guy. But he'd never gotten over Missy leaving.

Well, in all actuality, he'd never really gotten over Missy seducing Billy into bed before she left. Casey Joe had found her goodbye note, gone straight to his brother's place—distraught and in need of his family—and walked in on Missy getting dressed while a drunk Billy slept it off. The fight between the brothers was ugly enough to land them both in the county jail for a day or two. The feud ranged from mild to severe over the years since then, only really ending when Billy drank himself to death about six months ago.

Dad never recovered from Missy leaving or his brother's betrayal, but more than anything, the decades-long feud had been the worst. Casey Joe may have hated what Missy started between him and his brother—and hated even more that Billy let himself be pulled into her game—but mostly, I think Dad just missed his brother.

And now Billy was dead and Casey Joe wasn't taking it all that well.

Henry had taken over the bar for Dad back when he'd turned twenty-one. He was good at his job, enjoyed it, and kept the family's nest egg growing fat while giving a few locals steady jobs.

As a child, I'd spent most of my time between the orchard, The Juicy Peach general store, and the roadhouse —playing, doing homework, doing chores. During my teen years, I'd officially worked in the orchard and store. Unofficially, I'd also gotten paid on the side for part-time work at the roadhouse.

My adult years found me working at all three family businesses in addition to being the handyman of Haven Grove. I'd recently added massage services to my repertoire—mostly advertising my availability on sites populated by gay men, but also putting up a standard entry in the Haven Grove and surrounding area's business directory. Yes, I offered the standard run-of-the-mill relaxing and completely innocent massages to a wide variety of clients.

But for my male clients, I also offered the both-of-us-are-getting-a-happy-ending type of massage. And why not? Getting paid to give a massage, while having the added bonus of sex if the client opted into it, was easy and enjoyable money. Everything was consensual and agreed upon ahead of time, and I made sure my clients knew I was very serious about safety all around.

All of that to say, I had a lot going on. But that was fine by me because I liked to stay busy. Downtime wasn't something I really knew what to do with. If I wasn't working on *something*, I felt like I was wasting time.

So, adding the orchard and the general store to my list of things to do hadn't exactly been in my plan, but what was I supposed to do?

When Billy died, Dad had basically said good riddance and wanted to sell the orchard and The Juicy Peach. Dad wasn't doing all that great. He wasn't *sick*—at least, not physically. He'd kinda let himself go and his mental health wasn't fabulous. But mostly, I didn't think he could reliably take over either business his brother had been running—albeit poorly most recently—for decades. Not because Dad wasn't capable, just because I didn't think his heart was in it.

Henry and I had talked Dad out of selling by appealing to his sense of loyalty to the family name. His desire to have money to live on didn't hurt either.

That was how I'd agreed to take over where Billy had left off.

And it had been a damn mess.

The Juicy Peach needed repairs, a good cleaning, and major work when it came to keeping up-to-date stock ordered and the shelves filled. The books were a whole other story and kept me in a haze of numbers for several days until I finally felt I had them fairly close to balanced.

The peach orchard itself was our biggest money maker. We sold peaches by the bushel to grocery chains near and far. And we had a steady flow of locals and tourists who came to Haven Grove every year to snatch up pecks of peaches, whether our pre-picked ones or the you-pick variety. Add in all the peach goodies we sold at The Juicy Peach—pies, tarts, crumbles, peach tea, syrups, salsas; you name it, we probably had it—and the orchard was definitely what put the Riggs family on the map.

But when I'd taken over for Billy, I quickly realized that, not only was the store and the orchard a mess in a business sense, but the orchard also had some problems of a natural variety.

Whether Billy had known and didn't know what to do or just didn't care, a handful of the trees had bacterial spot. I wasn't an expert on peach tree diseases before, but I'd read enough since taking over to know bacterial spot had the potential to wipe out an entire orchard.

Luckily, I'd noticed it early enough and acted quickly. There was no guarantee, but I had high hopes the spray I'd used to treat the trees would work and we'd have a bumper crop come summer.

My phone buzzed as I said goodbye to Henry. My brother and I were close—as different as we were the same—we kinda had to be. I mean, I guess we didn't *have* to be close, but watching your mom walk away tended to pull two kids together. Henry and I fought, we definitely disagreed on a lot, but in the end, I knew he'd have my back. No questions. And I'd do the same for him.

My brother just rolled his eyes and shook his head as I grinned at the ClickC*ck message from User54321. Henry knew he wasn't going to change me, but that didn't mean he'd stop giving me shit for my no-strings-attached random hookup ways.

User54321: How about coffee? Glazed Buns Bakery?

Meeting at a public place was a good sign. Some men were looking for trouble and some were just plain stupid when they offered up a room number at the motel on the outskirts of town or agreed to have someone show up at their home.

The Glazed Buns Bakery was a local place with excellent coffee and amazing baked goods—they used our peaches and supplied us with stock during the season—and I'd quickly be able to size up this guy with the generic username and sexy-as-fuck silver-fox beard.

> Me: Sounds good. Can you do 4:00?

Grinning when Username54321 confirmed 4:00, I jumped in my truck and drove like a bat out of hell to the little farmhouse I called home between The Juicy Peach and our sprawling orchard. A quick shower and prep were in order if I lucked out and got this guy to head to the motel with me. Hell, if the vibe was right, I'd bring him to my place—which reminded me, the sheets needed changed—and maybe even let him spend the night before he went on his merry way.

My place was an original build and homey. Wood floors, traditional farmhouse kitchen, gorgeous staircase, and a lot of antique furniture my family had bought decades ago.

I wasn't much of a decorator, but the place looked pretty nice. And I kept it clean and tidy.

As I stripped the bed, I had a passing thought of what it would be like to meet someone and build a relationship. It wasn't the first time I'd wondered about seeking something more serious, but every time I thought about trying to create a future with a man I loved, I found myself nearing panic mode.

He'd leave.

Just like my mom.

If I ever gave my heart to someone, he'd rip it from my chest and obliterate it.

I wasn't good enough to convince Missy to stay.

If my own mother didn't even love me enough, how could I expect some guy to love me enough to commit to a whole future with me?

No, that was why it was for the best that I just kept things random and casual. No dating, no emotions, no strings.

Quick, easy, no risk of falling in love.

Because loving someone meant getting hurt.

And I'd had enough of that to last a lifetime.

By the time the bed had fresh sheets and I'd cleaned up and prepped, it was nearing four o'clock. I headed out of the gray-blue farmhouse, inhaling deeply of the orchard flowers as I neared my truck and couldn't help the feeling of contented satisfaction and excitement.

I didn't need a big city, a flashy car, a top-level corporate job, or a ring on my finger.

I had a great life in Haven Grove. My old truck was sensible and ran just fine. I loved having my brother and my dad so close. I would have hated wearing a suit or working in an office.

Sure, maybe my heart sometimes longed for love, but I knew better than to open up to something that would just end up falling apart.

Glazed Buns was quiet when I made my way to the counter. Two of Haven Grove's sweetest old women sat in a booth near the window and a teen with one earbud in washed tables. Not seeing anyone who could be Username54321, I headed to the counter and ordered a coffee.

Part of me wanted to get one for my date-who-wasn't-a-date, but it seemed too date-ish and presumptuous. What if he didn't care for coffee? Maybe he wanted tea.

As I overthought the situation and sipped my coffee, the bell over the bakery door jingled and my entire world shifted on its axis.

Forget Username54321.

Who needed an anonymous potential hookup when your living, breathing teen-years crush just waltzed back into town?

Chapter 2
Lance Ingram

WHAT THE HELL WAS I DOING?

I stared at my grayish-green eyes in the rear-view mirror of my late-model Ford truck. Haven Grove had been home up until about eight years ago and now I was back.

I'd been back in town a few days and I knew without a shadow of a doubt this was where I'd spend the rest of my life.

I had my old truck back.

Mom had handed me the keys to the Sweet & Creamy Dairy Palace—the Ingram family's ice cream shop my parents had opened the year I was born.

Mom and Dad ran the place for forty-four years. Then Dad left for the city eight years ago because he and Mom were done with being married. When Dad broke his leg, and my wife's father was diagnosed with a terminal illness, I had no choice but to move to the city with Kim to help both of our fathers.

Dad healed up fairly quickly, met some lady at physical therapy, and moved in with her. Kim's dad fought the disease for four years, but the prognosis had never been good. His slow death had been excruciating to watch.

Kim had made no secret of hating Haven Grove. Moving to the city had been perfect for her, but it had done nothing for our marriage. When her dad died and left her a huge chunk of money, she stuck around for two years. Then she announced she'd been cheating on me and she wanted a divorce.

What did it say about our marriage that I wasn't at all surprised or even upset? The fact she was the one leaving was almost a relief because I didn't have to finally pull the plug. I'd loved her at one point, hadn't I? I should have been sad to see our marriage end.

But in all honesty, all I could think about was how I'd tell my dad I wanted to go back to Haven Grove.

Over the next two years, I did nothing but miss my home and my old friends. I attempted to date, but the spark was never there. I finally admitted to myself I wasn't straight—I didn't know exactly *what* label fit me, maybe no label, but I knew straight wasn't where my sexuality landed.

When Dad told me Mom had called and asked if he thought I'd be willing to come to Haven Grove and help with the ice cream shop, I'd nearly fallen to my knees and wept. I wanted it so badly—I'd owned and run a very successful ice cream place in the city over the eight years I was there, but it didn't hold a candle to how much I wanted to be back in Haven Grove. Back to my roots.

The little midwestern town held my heart in a tight

grip and the moment my dad told me Mom needed me, I knew it was exactly where I wanted to be.

"But what about you?" I'd asked my dad.

He'd smiled and slapped me on the back. "Susan and I are moving to Florida. We're too old for city living. My bad leg needs the warmth and sunshine. Your momma needs you—we may not be together anymore, but I don't want her working herself to the bone to run the Sweet & Creamy. If you're willing to take it on—"

"I am," I'd said quickly.

He'd chuckled. "I'm sure Lucy would be pleased as punch to hand it over to you. If not, maybe you can help her get it ready to sell."

"Mom did *not* say she was selling, did she?"

"She said she would if you weren't willing to take over —and if I agreed to the sale," Dad explained.

"I'm taking over. There's nothing I've ever wanted more." The Ingram family name had been synonymous with ice cream since before I was born. Just like Haven Grove, the Sweet & Creamy was in my blood.

"Well, get yourself packed up then, boy."

I'd left fairly quickly, knowing I'd come back later to finalize everything. Kim had the house. I'd been living at Dad's place—he spent the majority of his time at Susan's anyway. My car wasn't much to look at, but I could easily sell it once I got to Haven Grove.

When I arrived, Mom hugged me and said she was happy to have me home. Told me I'd done good by taking care of Dad, but now it was her turn to have me in her life again. She'd moved out of the apartment over the shop several years ago, so I had an immediate place to live.

The ClickC*ck app I'd downloaded on my phone back in the city—and never really followed through on meeting up with any guys—had buzzed with a notification almost the moment I stepped foot in Haven Grove. Another user was nearby.

The profile picture for *HornyInHavenGrove* showed only a nice chest with sandy blond hair under an old leather jacket, the very edge of a tattoo peeking enticingly from around the man's belly button. Suddenly, I wanted to see more. More of the chest, more of the tattoo, more of that man.

It was absolutely ridiculous to even consider starting something up with a local when I was back in town for good.

Right?

And then he'd messaged me.

We'd spent a few days chatting about anything and everything. I'd never talked with a guy so effortlessly—it seriously felt like I'd known him my whole life.

By the time we'd agreed to meet for coffee at the Glazed Buns Bakery, I'd decided I wanted something more serious than a hookup with this guy. Yeah, I knew the ClickC*ck app was designed for quick, easy, no-strings-attached sex. I also knew I was stubborn, and I wasn't going to just hook up with this guy if I could keep from it.

A hookup with a local in a small town—especially when you planned to stay there for the rest of your life and run one of the town's most popular businesses—was a bad idea.

Dating a local in that situation maybe wasn't the *best* idea, but it was a lot less messy than random sex.

Right?

That was what I kept telling myself every time I questioned the idea.

You don't have a ton of experience with having sex with men.

Making out, a few blow jobs, and a couple fairly awkward nights don't really count.

Maybe you should look into dating some women?

Is getting involved with someone the moment you get back to town even smart? You've got the business to think of.

Nope.

I wasn't going to back down.

At fifty-three, I maybe didn't know myself completely, but I knew what felt right and I knew what I wanted. HornyInHavenGrove was different from all the other guys I'd chatted with on ClickC*ck. I wanted to meet him, see if the vibe was the same in person, and then go from there. If I had my way, he'd agree to a date by the end of the week.

I had no concerns about the Sweet & Creamy Dairy Palace. The Ingram family had made the most amazing homemade ice cream for over fifty years. We supplied local restaurants and businesses, we'd never had an hour of the day go by without at least five people in line to order—ten to twenty deep was the usual, and I already had some ideas to liven things up and increase sales.

Plus, I was taking over the shop, not the production facility. We made our ice cream on-site for the shop and local businesses, but the larger facility took care of the bigger orders for restaurants across the country. Running the shop was something I could do blindfolded.

Tomorrow, I'd meet with Casey Joe Riggs and talk to

him about a business relationship in addition to our life-long friendship. Aside from leaving Mom eight years ago, leaving my best friend had been the toughest. Casey Joe and I went way back and I hated leaving him and his boys. Those three had been through hell and back and I considered them family. When I left, I honestly wondered if Billy and Casey Joe would end up killing each other.

My best friend wasn't a texter and he didn't much care to talk on the phone. We exchanged a few emails over the eight years I was away from Haven Grove, but it wasn't the same as sitting on the back patio with a beer and the firepit, shootin' the shit, and enjoying the sounds of a small town on a summer night.

I chuckled to myself and shook my head.

Here I was, fifty-three years old and excited as fuck to be back home.

Using a damn hookup app with the hopes the guy wanted to try dating—knowing full well he'd likely laugh me all the way back to the city.

Making so many plans for meetings and merchandise and partnerships that I'd likely find myself busier in Haven Grove than I ever was when I ran a popular ice cream shop in the city.

Again, I asked myself, what the fuck was I doing?

Unfolding my six-foot frame from the truck, I caught a glimpse of my reflection in the window of Glazed Buns Bakery. The dark gray t-shirt stretched nicely over my broad chest—I didn't toil away at the gym hour after hour, but I thought I wore my age well. The worn jeans fit me just right. And the work boots were the perfect finishing touch. Kim had hated my silvering hair and constantly asked me to shave my beard, but I'd embraced the way the years painted silver through my hair. And I liked my beard. Period.

The bell over the door jingled when I walked into the bakery.

The scent of sweet cinnamon and coffee hit me first.

But what nearly took me to my knees—what had me forgetting every single thought of the man I was supposed to meet up with—was the guy sitting in the back corner.

I hadn't seen him in eight years, but I would have recognized Hudson Riggs anywhere.

He'd been gorgeous at twenty-five and he was breathtaking at thirty-three.

I'd been by Casey Joe's side—helping with Henry and Hudson, helping with the roadhouse, even helping Billy with the orchard when I could—ever since Missy screwed them all over.

Often, I was the buffer between Casey Joe and the boys. If they got in trouble and Casey Joe yelled for too long, too loudly, I stepped in. When the boys wanted something and Casey Joe said no without even considering, I stepped in. When the boys forgot a chore and panicked their dad would find out, I stepped in.

Leaving Haven Grove had been difficult for several reasons.

The Riggs family had been one of the hardest things to leave.

I didn't regret leaving. I knew my dad needed my help. I knew Kim and her father needed me. And being away had helped me truly find myself.

But I was home now. For good.

And staring at Hudson Riggs like you want to eat him alive is a very bad way to start your time here over again.

Shaking my head, and pushing away the thoughts of how fucking hot Hudson looked—reminding myself that Casey Joe didn't know I wasn't straight and the man would murder me, cut me to pieces with a spoon, and bury me in the orchard never to be found again if I got involved with his son—I checked my watch.

Aside from the teen washing tables and two ladies in a booth, Hudson was the only person in the bakery. I could catch up with him while I waited for *HornyInHavenGrove*.

Maybe I could get a read on how he thought Casey Joe would react to me bringing up a business partnership with the Riggs family peaches and the Ingram family ice cream. My best friend hadn't wanted to mix business and friendship all those years ago—and Mom hadn't been on board either—but maybe things would be different now.

I waved and smiled while pointing toward the counter.

Hudson returned the smile and glanced out the window. He must have been waiting for someone too.

With my steaming cup of black coffee, I made my way to Hudson's table.

He stood and pulled me into a friendly hug.

"Good to see you, man," Hudson said. "I'm meeting someone, but I've got a few minutes. Sit down if you've got time. What brings you back to town?"

"Mom was done with the shop and I was done with the city," I said, taking a seat across from Hudson. "I'm back for good."

"No shit?" Hudson said. He glanced at his phone

again. "I just saw Lucy the other day, she didn't say anything about you coming home."

"Honestly, depending on the day, she might not have known," I explained. "It was all pretty quick. Catch me up on everything," I said.

Hudson cocked a sandy blond brow and smirked. "Catch you up on eight years of what's been going on since you walked away?"

The jab was sharp and I kicked myself. I knew Hudson had a lot of trauma after the way Missy Riggs had left her family. "I didn't leave to stay gone. Some things needed tending to, but I always had plans to come back."

"Yeah, well," Hudson said dismissively. "I'm sure Kim will be dragging you away again as soon as possible." For some reason, Hudson had never really liked my ex-wife— even back when we'd been dating and just married, he'd always seemed to dislike her. Looking back, knowing what I knew now about the woman I'd married, I couldn't blame the kid. Kim hadn't been the nicest person. Beautiful and successful, yes. Life of the party, yes. Nice? Not even close.

"That chapter of my life is over," I said. "Kinda writing a new one now—maybe a whole new book."

Hudson's brows shot up. "Maybe it's you who should be filling me in on the last eight years."

Chuckling, I sipped my coffee and checked my watch. "Went to the city to take care of Dad and Kim's father. Dad recovered from the broken leg; Kim's father fought cancer for an excruciating four years. After he died, she got a lot of money, announced she'd been cheating on me, and wanted a divorce. I gladly gave it to her, stuck around for a while longer because Dad needed me, and jumped at the chance to come home when Mom said she was done running the Sweet & Creamy." My eyes met Hudson's over the rim of my cup. "Your turn."

There was that smirk again. "Um, nothing nearly as soap opera-ish as that," he teased. "Dad and Billy continued their feud. They did their usual working together—or working *around* each other—and grousing the whole time. Billy kept drinking, nearly destroyed the orchard and store with it. He finally drank himself to death about six months ago. Dad pretends like it doesn't bother him, but it does. I think losing his brother when Missy pulled her shit fucked him up worse than watching her walk away. He said he wasn't running the orchard or store and started talking about selling. Henry and I convinced him to let me take over." Hudson shrugged. "So, Dad helps where he can and when he feels like it. Henry runs The Roadhouse and I'm now the proud owner of a peach orchard and general store that may sink despite my best efforts."

I blinked. "Wow, that's...well, it's a lot. Hate to hear it about Billy, but can't say I'm surprised." I checked my watch again. "Looks like I'm being stood up."

Hudson chuckled. "Same. Fifteen minutes late and no contact seems a bit rude."

The teen bopped over to our table as we spoke, popping her gum. "Yeah, so, we're closing early today for an event. You don't have to leave yet, just thought I should let you know."

Giving her a nod, I glanced toward Hudson. "Any chance you wanna get out of here? I planned on talking to

Casey Joe about some ideas I had for a business partnership—cross-promotion type stuff—but now I guess I need to talk to you," I said. I didn't hate the idea.

Hudson cocked his head. "I'm down to listen to ideas. At this point, the orchard and store—and me—need all the help we can get." He tapped his phone. "Just let me tell this guy I'm gonna head out."

I pulled out my phone to let *HornyInHavenGrove* know I wasn't going to be able to meet after all. A couple quick words to explain—I honestly didn't feel bad about canceling since he hadn't even shown up—and I hit send.

Two things happened at once. My phone vibrated in my hand to indicate a new message and Hudson's phone chimed with the unmistakable sound of ClickC*ck.

> HornyInHavenGrove: Sorry, man. Looks like you're late and I just had something come up. Maybe another time.

I stared at my phone, trying to make sense of what I was seeing.

Hudson breathed out a low, "No fuckin' way."

Something clicked and I jerked my head up.

Our eyes met.

Confusion, curiosity, hope, and lust.

Refusing to cling to the hope and completely ignoring the lust, I huffed out a chuckle.

Hudson cocked a brow. "So, it looks like maybe you

didn't tell me everything that happened in the last eight years."

My face must have held a question—couldn't blame me, my brain was struggling to catch up.

He waved his phone. "ClickC*ck is an app for guys to hook up with guys. True, they may be bi, pan, gay, or even straight and sneaking around, but when you left here you were definitely sleeping with a woman. What happened?"

When I didn't blink, Hudson cringed.

"Sorry, that's invasive and insensitive. I was just some kid—"

"You were twenty-five," I said.

"True, but you'd known me as just some kid my whole life, it wasn't like you owed me any sort of explanation of your sexuality. It's not my business if you're gay or bi or pan or—" He cocked his head and studied me. "I can't see you cheating and sneaking around."

"I'm not."

"Not what?"

"Cheating and sneaking around." I ran a hand over my face. Had I really arranged a random hookup on an app only to find out I'd propositioned my best friend's son?

Fuck.

Even better, I wanted to talk my hookup into at least one date so I could get to know him better.

Get to know the guy better when I'd known him since birth?

To be fair, you don't know the person he is now.

I pinched the bridge of my nose. "I'm sorry."

Hudson frowned. "For what? Being the real you? Fuck that, man. Best thing I ever did was come out all those years ago. You were one of three people who supported me, and you did it better than Dad did, that's for sure. Doesn't matter if you've got it all figured out. Talk about it or don't, but I'm here if you want to."

I glanced at him. Hudson had always been unashamedly himself while being a supportive, listening ear to others. I'd seen him listen for hours while painting a widow's house. Or tinkering on old Mr. Johnson's truck. Or planting a row of green bean plants. He wasn't one to judge or push, he'd always been that way.

Suddenly, I wanted to pour it all out. The slow realization that women did it for me, but men did too—often even more. The constant wondering if it was just a mid-life crisis in my fifties. The inner argument of wanting a label to sort myself out and make everything into a nice, neat package while thinking that no specific label really fit me.

"No," I said instead. "I'm sorry for trying to hook up with you the first week I got back in town."

"To be fair, I tried to hook up with you too," Hudson said with an easy grin.

I ran a hand over my face.

Hudson leaned forward on his elbows. "Is it the first week back in town part that's bothering you? Would it have been better if you'd waited until week two? For propriety's sake?"

Huffing out a chuckle, I shook my head. "I see some things haven't changed."

Hudson shrugged and swigged the last of his coffee. "No reason to make things weird, might as well laugh it off."

We stood and gathered our trash before making our way toward the trashcan and the door.

"I mean, it *is* a little weird," I said. "You're my best friend's son."

Holding the door open for me, Hudson's hand brushed across my lower back as I walked past him. A jolt of awareness zinged through me, warm and electrifying.

"Wasn't planning on letting Dad get involved," Hudson whispered at my ear when we reached my truck.

He was too close, too fucking magnetic, too…just too *Hudson*. The scent of Irish Spring, something citrusy, and just *man* teased my senses.

I'd never thought of him in a sexual way, but that was then. Back before I'd recognized my attraction to men. Before I returned to the town I planned to make my forever home. Before I'd met Hudson Riggs as a man and not just the boy I'd known all those years ago.

Grasping onto the red flag and stepping out of the danger zone, I moved closer to my truck with a grunt. "Casey Joe's not getting involved because there's nothing to get involved with."

Hudson's eyes went wide and then his face fell. "What? Come on. It can be your welcome home party. I promise I'm the perfect hookup, I never ask for seconds. Dad won't hear a single word from me."

It was my turn for wide eyes. "You think quick, easy, no-strings sex with a guy you've known your whole life—a guy who is now living in the same town and very likely working close with you—is a good idea?"

Hudson shrugged. "I know I don't do relationships. And I know you already left once. I'll take my chances."

His challenge and insinuation shot right through me and I stepped closer, crossing my arms over my chest. "I'm home. To stay. And I'm not lookin' for something quick and easy." Nodding my chin toward the coffee shop, I said, "I had every intention of asking that guy out on a real date. Enjoyed talking to him so much, I wanted to see if the connection was there in real life."

"I don't date."

"Looks like we've found ourselves at an impasse. You don't date and I'm not interested in one-and-done, especially not with someone I'll be seeing on the daily." Why the hell did it sound like I was challenging Hudson to *date* me? I had absolutely *no business* getting involved with Casey Joe's son in any way other than work-related.

Hudson smirked. "Impasse. Yeah." He studied me. "Guess we're just working together, then."

My heart stuttered. Relief? Disappointment? I needed to get my shit together. "Guess so."

"It's a shame, really," Hudson drawled as I turned to get in my truck.

Giving him a sideways glance I asked, "What is?"

He let his gaze travel up and down my body, heat trailing over my skin as his eyes gobbled me up. "You're hot as hell. I thought my teenage wet dreams were about to come true."

My face heated and I sputtered. "You didn't...you weren't...did you..."

Hudson laughed. "Come on, Lance. You had to know I was panting after you from about sixteen on. Back then, it was just horny teen shit. But I'm thirty-three damn years old. We're not the same people we were back then.

Getting hot and sweaty with some good ol' fashioned sex isn't going to hurt anyone." He shrugged. "I'm just saying, we're consenting adults. There's a whole lot of fun to be had."

My brain was about to short-circuit. "But only once?"

Hudson considered me. "Maybe I'd make an exception for you. Maybe I'd allow repeats on a semi-regular basis."

My dick begged me to agree, my head screamed *danger, danger,* and my heart stuck out its bottom lip in a pout. "Then we're right back where we started. I want more than casual booty calls and no-strings, friends-with-benefits."

"With me?" Hudson challenged.

No.

Yes.

Fuck.

"Does it matter?" I asked, my back ramrod straight. "You want something completely different than what I want. Add in the fact Casey Joe would murder and wood-chipper me all over the orchard as fertilizer and I think we have our answer." I gestured toward his truck. "Now, are we going to look into this business arrangement or not?"

Hudson studied me for a long moment. "Let's do it. Just know, the offer still stands. I'm good for easy and casual. Maybe you can take me up on the offer before you head back to the city."

"I'm not going back," I said through gritted teeth.

"Mmhm," Hudson hummed.

"Meet me at the Sweet & Creamy," I said, yanking open my door. "And my offer still stands too."

Hudson sneered. "Dating?" he scoffed. "No, thank you. Not my style."

If I hadn't known what he'd been through with his mom, I probably wouldn't have picked up on Hudson's avoidance tactics. He didn't date, he didn't get close to people. Probably thought if he didn't let himself get attached, he couldn't get hurt like when his mom left.

Not that it mattered. I wasn't dating Casey Joe's son. I most definitely wasn't having no-strings-attached sex with him.

So, overall, Hudson was doing me a favor.

Actually, we were saving each other from a heap of trouble.

Business partners only was definitely the way to go.

I'd just have to get used to being around him and not getting distracted. Hudson had a perfect ass, killer smile, and snarky attitude all rolled into one.

It wouldn't be *that* difficult working with a permanent hard-on.

I gritted my teeth and tried to ignore the headache coming on.

Chapter 3
Hudson

As I followed Lance to his family's ice cream shop, I made a decision.

I wasn't going to give up on getting him in my bed.

Maybe it was a disaster in the making, but Lance Ingram had fueled my dreams as a teen, had been the epitome of sex-on-legs in my early adult years, and was silver-fox gorgeous now. I wasn't sure where he placed himself on the sexuality spectrum, but the fact he was on ClickC*ck was enough for me.

One night.

That's all I wanted.

I didn't buy the whole *I'm home for good* game.

He left.

He stayed gone nearly a decade.

Yeah, he was back, but he'd get bored of small-town living after all that time in the city. It was just a matter of time before he finished sprucing up the Sweet & Creamy, handed it off to someone else for a profit, and hightailed it out of town.

And I wanted a piece of him before that happened.

What happens if he stays? Might get weird. What if once turns into something more? He seemed pretty determined.

I shook my head as I pulled into a parking spot next to Lance on Main Street. I wouldn't let it happen. I'd had more than my fair share of hookups and *never* felt anything for any of them.

Sure, I'd had a crush on Lance back in high school.

Even pined a bit for him in my early adult years.

But he'd fled to the city and I'd written him off. Hadn't even given the guy a single thought in eight years. That had to be proof I wasn't *into* him, wasn't gonna fall for him or any shit like that.

I just wanted a night or two of sweaty, dirty fun.

Then we'd go on with our lives—which likely would mean Lance would be back to his big-city-life before the peach trees bloomed again.

I could live with that.

And if he demands a date in exchange for the sex?

Slamming my truck door, I chewed on that one for a bit. I didn't date. Period.

Lance unfolded his six-foot frame from his truck, and I bit my lip. The pretty silver hair sparkling in the sunlight, those jeans that fit his perfect ass like a glove, the crow's feet at his eyes when he squinted against the brightness.

How good would we look together? Our builds were similar, and I could picture our long limbs tangled, our bodies pressed together.

True, I didn't date.

But for a chance at Lance Ingram, my gay ass might just be willing to go to dinner.

The Sweet & Creamy Dairy Palace had been around since before I was born. Set up like the quintessential old-fashioned ice cream shop. Black and white checkered floor, original dark wood cabinets, shelves, and furnishings. Swivel stools at the bar. A row of booths with red and black cushions. Ten small, round tables designed to seat up to four. And one large, round table in the back for a party of ten.

The freezer, complete with glass windows where customers could see the ice cream and pick their flavor, held up to six varieties of ice cream at a time. Old-fashioned scoopers, glass dishes and milkshake glasses, and red and white striped straws completed the look. Shakes were mixed by hand with old-fashioned mixers. Waffle cones were made on-site. Sugar cones, cake cones, and to-go cups were all designed to spark nostalgia.

"Damn," I said, taking a deep breath. "You could have blindfolded me and I would have known exactly where I was." I ran my hand over the bar top. "You're keeping the soda fountain, right?"

Lance smirked. "Yeah, it's one of the main draws. You still like a vanilla Coke float?"

"If it's a real vanilla Coke, not the new stuff."

"Only real vanilla syrup here."

I grinned, my mouth watering at the thought of the sweet concoction.

Or maybe I was drooling over how fucking *fine* Lance was. He was gorgeous eight years ago, but indescribably handsome now.

He gestured for me to follow him behind the bar.

Twenty minutes later, Lance had walked me through the ice cream shop's inner workings and we settled in the back office to discuss his ideas.

He studied me over his desk, long frame stretched out in the chair. "What is it you have against dating?"

"When did you decide you're gay?" I shot back.

Lance just stared at me for a bit. "We can trade," he offered. "I don't know that *gay* is the right word. I'm attracted to men and women both, *people* really, maybe masculine slightly more than feminine." He shrugged. "But random, casual sex with strangers isn't my thing."

I cocked a brow. "Then ClickC*ck is the wrong app for you."

He pursed his lips. "Yeah, figured that out pretty quickly, but it didn't hurt to explore a bit."

He waited.

I waited.

Lance's steely gaze never wavered.

Huffing out a sigh, feeling like I was in the principal's office for throwing a rotten peach at Theo Rawlson in third grade, I shifted in my seat. "Dating means getting to know someone. It means getting close—I mean, I guess bad dates don't lead to that, but most people see the end game of dating as something permanent. I don't want permanent."

"Don't you?"

His question punched me right in the chest. "Nothing is permanent. That's the problem."

"Why not just be a serial dater instead of just a bunch of one-nighters?"

"First, it's not like I'm sleeping with a different guy every night of the year. Second, one night doesn't allow feelings to get involved. Dating opens things up to connections and shit. They're going to leave eventually. So, I just don't let it get to that point."

"Just fuck and leave?"

I shrugged. "If I don't stay, they can't leave."

The words echoed in my ears. It was the first time I'd spoken my little life motto out loud.

Lance's mouth turned down. "You deserve more than that."

"And you want to give me more? Ask Casey Joe for my hand in marriage and live happily ever after until you decide you're bored in Hick Town, USA and you leave? Again?"

Lance huffed. "This is my home, I'm not leaving."

"You did."

"That was then, I'm back to stay."

"So, you love me? Want to marry me? Think Dad will be fine with you fucking his son?"

He sighed. "I do love you—"

My eyes must have shown my disbelief because he amended his words.

"I've known you since the day you were born. You and your brother have always been special to me." Lance shifted in his seat. "I don't know what it is I feel toward you right now—it's very new and very different than anything I felt for you in the past. Different than anything I've ever felt for anyone at all. I can't say it's a happily ever after situation, but I'd like a chance to find out."

"And explain to Casey Joe?"

He ran a hand over his face. "Fuck, Hudson, I don't know. I just...I don't know...don't want to shut it down if it could be something."

"And I don't want to run the risk of being left behind again, so we're right back where we started. We've always been friends, that will have to be enough. Plus, we both know Dad would castrate you if he found out you were dickin' his baby boy." In all actuality, I wasn't sure how Casey Joe would react. Did he know Lance wasn't straight? Would that be a problem? I had a sneaking suspicion that Dad would be angry if Lance and I were doing the fuck buddy thing, but if he knew Lance wanted something serious, he might eventually come around. Of course, he'd likely kill us first and ask questions later, so it wouldn't really matter.

"I maybe haven't been around for a while, but I've known you your entire life. I know the type of man you are. I can't explain the draw, but it's there whether I understand it or not." Lance took a deep breath. "I just wish you'd allow yourself to be loved and happy the way you deserve."

"We've only been talking for a few days," I said, although Lance wasn't the only one to feel the pull.

"Which is why this whole situation has me all wound up. It's different. I'm not saying I'm *the one* to change your outlook on life—"

"My life is just fine." I cut him off and leaned forward in my seat. "Now, let's talk business. I've got a shit-ton of work to do with the orchard and the store, plus helping Henry at the bar. I don't have time to take on a huge amount of extra, so let's see what we can figure out."

The glint in Lance's eyes told me he wasn't done pushing this conversation, but he gave a slight smile and nodded as if he was willing to concede at least for the time being.

"I think the Sweat & Creamy Dairy Palace, The Juicy Peach general store, and Riggs Family Orchard need to combine their forces," Lance said.

I shrugged. "We already sell your ice cream at the store and you use our peaches every season."

"I think it needs to be more than that," Lance argued. "The place I used to run made good money, but when I partnered up with the mom-and-pop diner around the corner, both businesses saw a major profit increase."

Not gonna lie, the potential of increasing our profits—especially since the orchard's bottom line had taken a direct hit thanks to Billy's drinking and letting everything go—had me intrigued.

"Partnered up? How? What more could we be doing?" I asked.

Lance pulled a legal pad from his desk and slid it across to me. "Some of these are things we should have been doing from the beginning. Some are things Mom would have never gone for. We don't have to do every single item right away, but I think there's a lot we can do for each other."

I scanned the list.

Sell Roadhouse peach simple syrup at DP and Juicy.

Merchandise- sell at all three- t-shirts, stickers, mugs to start with.

Funny/play on words type things.

Canned peaches from Juicy to sell for ice cream toppings.

DP sells peach crumble in a jar to pair with ice cream.

Both places sell margarita and daiquiri mixes.

All three places have gift certificates available for purchase-customers can get all of them at one place instead of having to go place to place.

Offer discounts between Juicy and DP- bought ice cream at DP? Show receipt and get percent off a pie or crumble at Juicy.

With my head spinning, I brought my eyes up to meet Lance's. "Someone's been a busy brainstormer."

He smiled. "Just feels like we're losing out on business. Business means money."

"Wow, never thought of it that way," I deadpanned, smirking when Lance rolled his eyes. "What's this funny, play on words thing?"

"You know how certain businesses play on their name or what they sell to be funny with innuendo?"

I nodded, not completely following.

"Come on," Lance said, a hint of embarrassed frustration in his voice, "I can't be the only one who thinks *The Juicy Peach* and *Sweet & Creamy* are funny. Dairy Palace shortened to DP?"

For a brief second, I thought about playing dumb, but I put Lance out of his misery with a chuckle. "So, you want to slap some innuendo on t-shirts and hope a bunch of people with the sense of humor of teens and tweens will buy them?"

Lance's cheeks pinked, but he shrugged. "T-shirts, stickers, magnets, mugs—at least to start with."

"You have a list of these funny things?"

"Maybe a few, but we can brainstorm over lunch in the next few days."

I glanced at the list again. "Seriously, between the orchard, the store, the bar, and a handful of odds-and-ends type jobs I do around town, I don't have a lot of time to take on extra." Lance knew about my handyman side hustle from way back, but I wasn't about to tell him about the massage business. It wasn't *all* sexual, I did plain ol' massages just to loosen up muscles and help people relax, but I had a feeling he wouldn't be super excited to hear I'd added sex worker to my resume.

Lance cocked his head. "What do you do in your free time?"

Frowning, I shook my head. "Free time? Doesn't compute."

His brows shot up. "Free time. What you do to relax, rejuvenate, take time for you in the interest of your mental health and well-being?"

"I don't have time for any of that."

Lance continued to stare at me before a breath left him in a whoosh. "You're not joking, are you?"

"No. There's truly no time for me. I take care of jobs around town, I work at the orchard and the store trying to make sure they don't go under, I help Henry at the bar. When I'm not working, I pretty much have time to eat, shower, pay some bills, and go to bed. Sometimes I listen to a podcast in my truck—" I broke off. "What?"

He shook his head. "You're young. People my age have often figured out that working themselves to death isn't worth it. The youngins—younger than you even—are all about keeping their mental health a priority—sometimes to a fault, if you ask me. But you seem to be in that middle group that thinks there's some prize for constantly being busy and never taking a time out for *you.*"

I didn't really have anything to say to that.

Lance huffed. "I have several goals now that I'm back home and I just added another one to the list."

"What's that?" I'd be lying if I wasn't hoping he'd say he'd changed his mind and now wanted one dirty, sweaty night with me.

"I'm going to make sure you learn how to take a break," Lance said, one hundred percent serious. "Working yourself to death isn't a life."

I snorted. "I'm not working myself to death. I like to stay busy. Taking a break feels wasteful. If I'm not *doing* something, I get restless and anxious. It's easier just to keep going. I'm healthy and content, you don't need to worry about me." *Not like you'll be here that long anyway,* I thought, but I wasn't in the mood to ruffle Lance's feathers any more than I already had.

Again, Lance looked as if he wanted to argue, but he just tapped the notepad. "Can you do lunch tomorrow? Bring your best ideas."

I had a lunchtime massage the next day—just a regular one with a lady in town who had no clue about my *other* massage services. "Can't, I've got plans."

"Day after?"

I shook my head. "I'm actually pretty booked up for the next three or four days. How about Monday? In the evening? I can do like six at the bar." I'd be able to stay and help Henry after our meeting.

"It's Thursday," Lance said, frustration lacing his words.

"Take it or leave it."

"That works," Lance said.

"Sounds good. See you then."

"Careful."

I quirked a brow.

"Almost sounds like we've got a date."

I grunted and stood. "We have a meeting to discuss a business relationship while eating food. That's not a date."

Lance stood from his desk and stuck out his hand. "Either way, I'm looking forward to working with you, Hudson. I'm happy as hell to be back home and excited to increase business for both of us." We shook and made our way to the front door where we said our goodbyes.

I then proceeded to spend the next three days dreaming, overthinking, and fantasizing about Lance Ingram. I wanted him like no man I'd ever wanted, but it was more than that.

It was good to have him back in Haven Grove.

I was happy to be working with him—I'd liked his ideas and we had a good chance of making something really good with our businesses.

But more than anything, seeing Lance, spending even just that little bit of time with him, sparking a connection I hadn't even realized I'd been missing over the last eight years...all of it did something deep inside me. It was like I'd had a Lance-shaped hole in my life and hadn't even known it. From the moment he walked into Glazed Buns, something had changed.

I breathed easier.

Smiled more genuinely.

And looked forward to the future.

It wasn't like I could let any of that shit go anywhere—obviously, I'd just be asking for trouble. But I wasn't going to lie. I liked the thought of Lance being home.

With me.

And wasn't that just a selfish, fucked-up, crash-and-burn disaster waiting to happen?

Chapter 4

Lance

I'D TAKEN MOM'S SUGGESTION AND SHUT THE ICE cream shop down for a few days to take inventory, clean, and get ready for a soft re-opening.

The Sweet & Creamy wasn't *dirty*—Mom would have never let it get that way—but there was a lot of reorganization to be done if I wanted it set up *my* way.

I spent a few very long days working on the shop.

At quittin' time on Sunday, I locked up, ran upstairs to the apartment I now called home, and took a quick shower. I'd called Casey Joe earlier to see if he wanted to do pizza and beer at his place. He'd agreed as long as I brought both.

Some things hadn't changed a bit.

When I pulled my truck in at Casey Joe's place, I saw my lifelong friend sitting on the front porch.

While time had been friendly to me—it wasn't a brag, I just knew I'd aged well—time and trauma had *not* been kind to him.

Casey Joe looked at least ten years older than our fifty-three. His eyes had lost the sparkle they'd had back when we were teens. When he stood, I took in the slumped shoulders, the slight limp, and the shadow of a few extra pounds around his middle. He wasn't completely gone to seed, but he needed to hit the gym if he was going to shape back up and start feeling better.

Grabbing the two pizza boxes and the twelve-pack of beer, I thought of all Casey Joe had been through since we were teens.

He loved his boys, but I knew he'd never planned on having kids and settling down so young. Missy leaving him with the boys was bad, but her sleeping with Billy before she left town was the real dagger. And to hear Hudson tell it, Casey Joe losing his brother recently—even though they'd never been the same after Missy fucked them all over—had been the worst.

Did I even know my best friend anymore?

What would he think if he knew I'd met up with Hudson through a hookup app for men who have sex with men? More so, what would he think if he knew I had all these crazy thoughts about Hudson? Would he care that I wanted to woo his son? Wanted to date him? Romance him into giving us a chance?

He'd likely think you've gone and lost your damn mind. You just met the guy and now you want a happily ever after?

Not true.

I'd known Hudson for his entire thirty-three years, saw him just about every damn day for twenty-five years before I went to help Dad in the city.

Sure, I'd just met him as a consenting adult outside of

our former relationship, but it wasn't as if he was a stranger.

Still, Casey Joe would probably think you were insane.

I sighed and hefted the beer against my hip. Maybe I was. But I'd wanted to delve deeper into the spark between me and HornyInHavenGrove long before I knew it was Hudson. Knowing it was him hadn't changed that.

Yeah, maybe the fact it was Hudson made it a little more challenging, but it didn't stamp out the spark I'd felt for him on the app. If anything, spending time with Hudson and chatting with him through text the last week had only flamed the sparks into an actual fire.

So, take him up on his offer of one-and-done and see where it goes.

Believe me, my dick was completely on-board with this idea.

But part of me felt like giving in to the one-time hookup was cheapening what might be between us.

Get some good sex and see where things go. Maybe Hudson is a terrible lay. Or maybe you'll coerce him with your magical dick, and he'll be putty in your hands as you convince him to spend forever with you.

I chuckled and shook my head as I made my way up the porch steps at Casey Joe's.

"How the hell ya been?" Casey Joe drawled, taking the pizza and beer from me. He placed them on the little porch table before pulling me into a hug and slapping me on the back.

"Good, good, how 'bout yourself?" The urge to say *You look good* or something equally false and ridiculous was strong, but I knew Casey Joe would call me on bullshit.

He took the swing and I took the folding lawn chair, praying it wouldn't fold under me. Casey Joe popped open a beer and took a bite of pizza before he spoke.

"Y'been gone a while," he said. That was the way Casey had always been. Not one to talk a lot, but direct and to the point when he did.

I nodded, grabbing my own beer and slice of pizza. "Yeah. Dad's leg healed pretty quickly, but Kim's dad suffered for a long time." He knew this from the emails we'd exchanged, but it was something easy to talk about. "Dad and Susan moved to Florida."

"And Kim ran off. Like they all do."

Swallowing a bite, I said, "They don't *all* run off—"

"Missy did. She fucked everything up."

"I know, man. I was here. She didn't deserve you and those boys."

Casey Joe chuckled, but there was no humor. "Maybe not—honestly, I know the three of us were better off without her in the long run—but she hurt my boys, she hurt me. Killed my brother."

Now, it was a known fact that Billy Riggs had been an alcoholic long before Missy fucked him and left town, but it didn't seem the right time to argue the fact. And maybe Casey Joe was right, maybe Billy's drinking got worse after Missy.

We were silent for a bit, then he spoke again. "So, you're stayin'?"

Nodding, I took a swig of beer. "I am. Back for good. Kim leaving helped me to figure some shit out about myself. One of the things I figured out is I'm not cut out for the city—this is my home; my heart is here—I'm not leaving again."

We each finished our beer and polished off the pizza before Casey Joe spoke again. "You seem different." He eyed me up and down. "All sophisticated and shit. Like, you're dressed how we've always dressed for small-town workin'—boots, jeans, t-shirt, all that shit," he motioned up and down to my clothes, "but it's all designer and fancy or somethin'."

I laughed. "Can't really get Wranglers at the stores in the city, had to make do with a little bit higher fashion."

"Well, y'look good."

"Thanks."

Casey Joe laughed. "Good to have you home. Thanks for not saying I look good. I know I look like shit. Just can't seem to care anymore." He gestured toward the general vicinity of the orchard. "Those boys are the only reason I ever kept going."

"How are they? The boys." A dangerous thrill rocketed through me as I thought of the way Hudson and I had reconnected. The images in my head of spending time with him in a way far, far outside of the relationship we used to have.

"As good as can be expected, I guess. Henry stays pretty quiet. Hudson is the social butterfly, but he has his own issues. Not sure either of them will ever find happiness..." he paused and huffed out a breath, "something else she took from us. I can't say I understand the two of them being *queer* and shit—" he broke off and held up a hand as if to stop a protest, "it's okay to use that word to describe them if it's not in a derogatory way—which it's not—and they both find it acceptable—which they do. The boys and I have talked about it." He accepted my nod and went on, "Anyway, can't say I understand it—Henry saying he likes girls *and* guys, Hudson liking guys—but I know I want my boys happy and healthy. Not sure they'll ever get that because she went and fucked them up." He sighed. "Hell, I probably did my fair share of fuckin' them up."

We were halfway through our second beers, Casey Joe's eyes focused on something far off in the distance.

"But you'd be okay with either of them being with a man? As long as they were happy?" I wondered if one day, down the road, we'd look back at this conversation as the first time I hinted to my best friend that I had a strong attraction—a draw like never before—to his son. Would Casey Joe remember me asking this and punch my lights out when he realized I'd been back in town only a few days when I'd decided to start courting Hudson?

Fuck.

I was playing with fire. I knew it—it wasn't smart; I should just forget about Hudson and move on—but an invisible string coiled in my gut, pulling me toward Hudson in a way I couldn't even begin to comprehend, much less explain.

Casey Joe grunted. "Like I said, can't say I understand it, but we've all been so fucked up, I just want them to have a chance at happiness. Chance I didn't get." He ran a hand over his face. "Damn, it's like you came home and all my melancholy shit came pouring out. Haven't talked so much in damn near eight years. Missed you."

"Missed you too. Missed this place."

Casey Joe squinted as he studied me. "It's not just the clothes and the fancy haircut—the silver is nice though, lot more of it these days—there's something else different about you." He cocked his head.

"Still the same ol' me," I said. "Just know myself a bit better now."

"Y'like yourself better the older you get?" he asked.

I nodded, the third beer making things a bit fuzzy. "I do."

Casey Joe grunted. "Me too. Wish I could go back and tell that kid a few things." He sighed. "But then I wouldn't have my boys and they're the only things that've made this life worth livin'." He popped open another beer and stood, walking to the edge of the porch. "Hell, I don't know. I wouldn't go back to all that shit, before or after Missy left, but I'm not sure I like this gettin' old shit either."

"Sometimes feels like the years are flying by," I mused. "Your boys can be happy." Slapping him on the back, I took another swig of beer. "You can too." Suddenly, Casey Joe's happiness was something I wanted to see. Needed to know he was okay.

I wasn't self-absorbed enough to think my presence back in town would be enough to make things better for my friend, but I hoped maybe I could help. Even if just a little. Casey Joe Riggs had been playing a shit hand he'd been dealt over three decades ago, it was time for a shuffle and re-deal. He deserved a chance to find his happiness.

We spent the next hour shooting the shit like we'd never been apart. Casey Joe said I was different, but he was too. Maybe it wasn't for the same reasons, but he'd changed. Not for better or for worse, just changed. Something I guessed we all did as the years went by.

An ache filled my chest. Fifty-three years gone. Fifty-three years...wasted? Misused? Had I missed the best years of my life in a marriage I regretted? Years lost thinking of myself one way, losing the chance at true love and happiness because I didn't even have the capacity to think of myself another way?

Fifty-three isn't ancient, for God's sake. You take care of yourself and you're healthy. Don't wallow in what you might have missed, look forward to what's to come.

My friend drank his beer, regret and misery evident in every cell of his being, and I wished I could help him look forward to something better. But I knew from experience that I couldn't force that on anyone. Casey Joe would have to come to that point himself. Until then, I'd just be the best friend I could be.

By sleeping with his son?

Fuck.

Part of me felt like a grade-A asshole for even contemplating taking that spark with Hudson and working to make it more. But the other part of me figured if something took shape between Hudson and me, it would be between two consenting adults and we'd deal with any fall-out if it was needed.

By fall-out, I meant Casey Joe.

And maybe Henry.

Would Henry be pissed I had a thing for his brother?

Would Casey Joe and Henry think I'd been perving over Hudson for decades?

Nothing could be further from the truth. I hadn't even

thought about looking at other dudes until about halfway through my eight years away. I definitely hadn't been drooling over Hudson all those years ago. It had taken the baggage of a shit marriage, missing home, the trauma of watching a person die slowly, and having Kim cheat on me before she walked away to push me toward the deep soul-searching that finally led to me recognizing that part of myself.

The me of now definitely remembered twenty-five-year-old Hudson as a gorgeous specimen when I left town, but the me of twenty-some years ago wouldn't have given a guy a second look—especially not a teenaged one.

The man I'd become—the man I'd finally accepted as the real me—wanted to cherish the past I had with the Riggs family, but more than anything, I wanted to build a future with them. Reconnecting with friends, learning to love each other as we were *now*.

And hopefully helping Hudson realize that loving someone didn't have to mean losing them.

If I don't stay, they can't leave. Hudson's words came back to me.

I definitely had my work cut out for me.

And who was I to think I could win him over? Show him relationships didn't have to hurt? A middle-aged divorced man who recently discovered his sexuality fell somewhere on the *not-straight* portion of the spectrum. What did I have to teach Hudson?

Not to mention the fact that maybe Hudson wasn't attracted to me in the same way. Was I being a total ass thinking that just because I'd felt a connection to the man, he did as well? There was a very good chance he felt none of what I felt.

But...

That invisible string coiled in my belly pulled, yearning for the man I'd spent days texting with and hours discussing our new business adventure.

I maybe didn't have a lot of experience with strong, loving relationships, but I knew what my gut said. Knew what my heart wanted. This wasn't infatuation or a crush. It had come on quickly, but it was as real as anything I'd ever felt.

And he'd felt something too. No one spends *that* many hours texting if all they wanted was sex. He maybe wanted sex, but there was more there.

Hudson and I were meant to be.

We'd needed a good chunk of time—say, thirty-three years—to get to a point where our connection could turn into something good.

And now we were here.

It was maybe quick, but it was the most *right* thing I'd ever felt.

I just needed to win Hudson over. Give him so much *good* that he had no option but to stay.

Then prove to him I wasn't going to leave.

Haven Grove was my home.

Hudson was my future.

I walked into the bar about twenty minutes 'til six the day Hudson and I were meeting to go over business shit. I'd had almost a full week of thinking about him and what I wanted from life now that I was back in Haven Grove.

That instant spark of connection we'd had through messages on ClickC*ck had been just enough to reignite the closeness we'd had in the past. I'd accepted that perhaps I was just lonely and horny—maybe the draw toward Hudson would ease once we'd had some time apart.

But we'd been texting from sun up to sun down over the past week and nothing had changed. If anything, the time away and the easy conversations had only fanned the flames.

Only made me want him more.

Want him as in all of him.

Not just for sex.

His heart, his body, his mind, all of it.

Yeah, I knew I could have him for sex at the drop of a hat, but I wanted more than that. I wanted to know what made him tick, wanted to know the man he kept hidden from everyone else.

Maybe you could have sex with him first and then work toward having more with him.

The thought had been running through my head ever since Hudson told me his offer stood. While I wanted more with him—and part of me feared he'd shut me out completely once we slept together—I wasn't sure involving sex in the situation was the best idea.

But on the other hand, I wasn't sure it was a *bad* idea either.

I'd decided we'd work together and see where things went.

"Look what the cat dragged in," a low voice rumbled as my eyes adjusted to the dim light inside The Riggs Family Roadhouse. The place didn't look any busier than usual and the bar was fairly empty for the time being.

The roadhouse was exactly what you'd expect from a small-town bar. Dark wood, a mix of tables and booths, windows covered in stained glass, a long bar with stools, and a line of every liquor imaginable lined up against the mirrored wall behind the bar. The original wood floor shone in the light of the stained glass and the hanging lamps over each table and the bar. The place did an amazing job of giving off homey and rough all at once.

Henry Riggs had a persona that screamed *stay away*, but he was mostly a big softie. He looked a lot like his brother —only slightly taller, somewhat scruffier, possibly a bit broader—but he'd always been the quieter one of the two. Henry spoke less than Hudson—or at least he always had back when I was around them day in and day out. He looked like the rougher and tougher of the two brothers, but those who really knew him—not more than a few people at most if I had to guess—saw the soft caretaker side of Henry. He'd always had a great sense of humor, his eyes sparkling with mischief and laughter when he was comfortable around a person.

Henry had made it his mission to take care of Casey Joe and Hudson from a very young age after Missy walked out on her family. He'd worked hard his whole life to bring in money, help his dad and brother, and keep the Riggs name on a pedestal in Haven Grove.

Looking at the man now, after eight years of being away, I saw the same old soft-spoken caretaker, his eyes bright with humor as he teased me. But Henry also looked…empty? Like something was missing. After knowing the brothers their entire life, I immediately thought that if Hudson was conquering his trauma with random, meaningless hookups, Henry was likely doing the opposite. Henry would be the type to avoid getting involved with people, avoid opening himself up to the potential hurt. Hudson did the same, but he thrived on the contact—he just kept all that contact at a double arm's-length distance.

"Henry," I said with a smile. A whoosh of air escaped me when he pulled me into a hug. "Good to see you."

"Grapevine has it that you're home for good," Henry said, releasing me from the bear hug and returning to his place behind the counter.

"Yep," I said, accepting the water he placed before me.

"And you're thinking about combining forces with the Riggs family," he said, those eyes sparkling.

"Yep." I couldn't help the grin. "Hudson and I are meeting to go over plans."

"I know."

I cocked a brow.

Henry shrugged. "Hudson's been chittering about it since you brought it up. He wants to act like he doesn't have time, but he's excited about it."

My chest filled with warmth. "Yeah?"

Henry nodded.

"And what about you? You think it's a good idea?"

The big guy slid a menu in front of me. "I think the store and your place will have a lot more opportunity to help each other out, but I'm down for figuring out how the roadhouse can fit into everything."

"I'll order dinner once Hudson gets here, but give me a Peach Sour for now." I took a long swallow of my water while Henry mixed my drink. "That peach simple syrup right there will be one of the biggest ways you can be involved. Everyone loves it, loves that it's made right here, loves to fancy themselves a mixologist at home in their kitchen with your peach syrup. We'll sell it at the shop—promo it as the perfect addition to a milkshake, with or without alcohol. I think, at least in the summertime, the roadhouse should offer peach ice cream along with other peach desserts. All three places will sell each other's gift certificates. Maybe you could add some Sweet & Creamy and Juicy Peach merchandise here and we'll do the same with Riggs' Roadhouse t-shirts and glasses." I took a sip of the Peach Sour Henry placed before me. "Damn, that's even better than I remember it. So, what do you think?"

"I'm in. I think it's a great idea. Kinda makes me wonder why we didn't do it earlier."

I shrugged. "Mom wasn't on board. Your dad didn't like the idea. Not sure Billy would have either—or at least he probably wouldn't have been able to follow through with it."

"Well, you've got Hudson all worked up about possibilities," Henry said. "The orchard and store kinda got thrust on him—he's worked at both his whole life, but being the sole person responsible for all of it...especially when Billy almost tanked it...has put a lot of stress on him. But he's keyed up with ideas."

"We had a pretty good talk. I trust him to work his ass off alongside me to make this work."

Henry fixed me with a look I couldn't decipher.

"What?"

"He told me about the way you met up," Henry said.

My heart caught in my throat. "Does that bother you?"

"What?"

"That I was on that app?"

"You know I'm bi."

I nodded.

"So, no, it doesn't bother me. I don't get the whole random hookup thing, but he seems to be happy with it."

I held up a hand. "We didn't hook up."

With a tiny grin, Henry said, "I know." He paused and I knew there was more he wanted to say.

I raised my brows and waited.

Henry cleared his throat. "He's been talking a lot about you."

"Good or bad?"

He shook his head. "Neither. Just talking. Like he doesn't want to sound too eager but can't help keepin' your name in his mouth."

My name in his mouth? Sweet jeezus. The picture that painted. "And you think it's a bad idea?"

Henry took a deep breath and blew it out slowly. "I think that Hudson needs someone to love him and take care of him. I think he needs to stop with the random sex and look for something real." He filled my water and nodded toward my glass. When I nudged the glass toward him, he took it, mixing another Peach Sour while he spoke. "I think it may be the stupidest thing either of you have ever done if you get involved in business and pleasure when you both plan to build futures here."

"But?"

Henry shook his head, a soft grin teasing his lips. "But...I also think Hudson's trying *real* hard to convince himself all he wants with you is a random hookup. I think he's fooling himself if he thinks knowing someone for thirty-three years can lead to a successful, no-strings-attached hookup. I think there's *way* too much history between the two of you. I think Dad will likely have your head."

I swallowed. Hard. "Gee, tell me how you really feel," I deadpanned.

Henry chuckled. "I have to say that it seems a bit quick," he hedged.

"It does, I'll agree." I took a sip of the sweet peach concoction. "On the flip side, we're not strangers. And we've spent more time talking and texting in the last week than I spoke to my ex in the whole last year we were together."

"Maybe it's one of those *when you know you know* type things. Can't say I've ever experienced it, at least not relationship-wise, but I've had the feeling regarding other things."

"Yeah, that's kinda the way I'm feeling. It just feels different. *Right* somehow."

"Main thing I know is Hudson has *never* talked about someone as much as he's talked about you." He frowned. "So, I guess what I'm saying is, if you think this could be something *real*, go for it. If you're not into him, not looking for anything other than one-and-done sex, don't get involved. He'd *say* he was fine with it. He'd swear it was what he wanted. But he has zero experience sleeping with guys he's known his whole life—I really don't think he could do casual with you and it would eat him up."

"I am."

Henry narrowed his eyes. "You are what?"

"Into him. But I don't do random and casual."

"Why were you on ClickC*ck?"

I huffed out a breath. "Figuring things out. Curiosity. Hell, at this point, maybe I should say fate had me create an account."

"So, what's your plan?"

I ran a hand over my face and chuckled. "Well, I'm a fish out of water here. Crappy marriage, cheated on, divorced, and I've only known I'm *not straight* for about four years. But I guess my plan is to woo him. Romance him? Convince him we're better together than apart? Show him that not everyone leaves?" Dropping my head onto my arms on the bar, I groaned. "Fuck, I have no clue."

When I finally pulled myself back up, Henry nodded, his face serious. "You'll have to be patient."

"I can do that."

"He may really fight you."

"That's okay."

He cocked his head. "Or, he may fall apart the moment he gets a sense of what it's like to be taken care of. Soon as he lets you in just a fraction, his walls might crumble. Honestly, could go either way."

"I'm here for good. I can be patient. I know it's insane how we met back up. The age gap, the fact I've known him his whole life, he's my best friend's son. All of it. But I don't know how to walk away from it. Don't know how to shut it off." I pinched the bridge of my nose. "Oh, god, the age gap. Is it too weird? Creepy? Fuck, Casey Joe is going to kill me."

Henry made a sound between a grunt and a chuckle. "Twenty years is one of those numbers that can seem like forever and nothing all at once."

"So, am I a creepy old man or not?"

"Nah, you're not old. And Hudson is a grown-ass man. He can decide who he likes and wants to spend time with. Some people might do a double-take...might talk a bit... but I know my brother has a good head on his shoulders. If he decides he wants to be with you, so be it."

I huffed. "And Casey Joe?"

Henry chuckled again and winced. "Well, Dad may be a different story all together. I'm thinking maybe you don't let on the two of you have something going on until you're both one hundred percent what you've got. That way, you can defend yourselves and show him it's real. If he catches you and neither of you can claim it's something more than sex, he's likely to be big-time pissed—worried about his baby boy being taken advantage of and whatnot. Even though he knows Hudson is an adult, Dad will strike first and ask questions later." Henry cocked his head, his eyes squinting as if thinking something over. "Not sure if you being his best friend and so close to us growing up will work in your favor or against it."

Groaning, I drained my drink. "Can't say you've helped me feel any better," I groused.

Henry just smiled.

I checked my phone. It was almost six. "Hey, listen, can you help me give Hudson a rough time?"

"I live to give my baby brother shit," Henry said, his eyes sparkling.

Five minutes later, the door opened and Hudson walked in.

Just like when I saw him again for the first time at Glazed Buns, my breath caught. He was so damn gorgeous. The sandy blond hair, those bright blue eyes, that ass encased in jeans that looked as if they'd been made especially for him. He exuded sex appeal, but Hudson also had an air of eager, clumsy puppy—all big feet and excitement—about him. Maybe it was because he was younger, maybe it was just his zest for life, but I loved it.

"Hey," Hudson said when he sat down next to me at the bar.

"Hey."

"Didn't know you had a date," Henry said with a smirk.

"Fuck you," Hudson said to his brother before turning to me. "And fuck you too. It's not a date."

I pulled out my phone and showed him the dictionary definition of a date. *A social or romantic appointment or engagement.*

Hudson scoffed and pulled out his phone, tapping aggressively. "Ha. First, this isn't *romantic*."

"Could be, if you'd let it," I murmured.

Hudson ignored me. "Second," he stuck his phone in my face, "similar words are appointment and meeting. This is a meeting. Nothing more." He leaned in close, his voice taking on a sultry quality. "Now, if you wanted to define date as *a consensual sexual engagement*, I'd be willing to accept."

I grabbed the menu and scanned the choices, hoping that thinking about French fries would help me ignore the heat roiling through me at Hudson's words. The way his warm, soft breath tickled against my skin.

"I'll have the Riggs burger, fries, ranch, and an unsweet tea," I said. They'd added a bit to the menu over the years, but the burger was a tried-and-true favorite.

"Damn man," Hudson teased. "How do you look so good eating like that?"

Basking in the compliment, but doing my best not to let it show, I stood and gestured toward a table as I said, "Balance is key. And I'll work it off at the shop or the gym."

"*The gym,*" Hudson echoed, "is in desperate need of someone new to run it. Really hoping they end up selling it to someone who is going to turn it around. Needs new equipment—hell, needs a whole damn makeover. It's like walking into a dungeon of rusty metal, old sweat, and hibernating fungus, and trying to work out."

Hudson told Henry he wanted the grilled lemon pepper chicken and sautéed vegetables, a salad with vinaigrette, and sparkling water.

Henry chuckled and flipped his brother off. "Your usual then?"

"Obviously."

We made our way to a booth in the far corner. The roadhouse had quite a few customers eating and talking, some just drinking and watching TV, but the booth was set away from everything enough to provide a bit of privacy.

I pulled a notebook and pen from my computer bag and glanced at Hudson. "Did you come prepared for brainstorming?"

His cheeks pinked. "Um, uh..."

"That's what I figured," I teased. Pulling out a second notebook and pen, I slid them across the table. "Let's do this."

Chapter 5
Hudson

WE'D BEEN CHATTING ON TEXT FOR AROUND A week and never once did it feel like Lance and I struggled to find things to talk about.

The damn weird draw to him I had would have been much easier to shrug off if things had been awkward between us when we met up in person to discuss the business venture.

But they weren't.

Despite the fact we'd reconnected over a hookup app, the lifetime between us eased any awkwardness. We chatted easily as we waited for our food, talking about folks around town as if we'd been meeting up for dinner once a week for our entire lives.

Being around Lance was so easy. I loved it and hated it all the same.

Loved it because I'd missed him more than I'd realized and having someone I used to be close with back in town to buddy up with was nice.

Hated it because I'd missed him more than I'd realized and having someone I used to be close with back in town making me want him more and more with each passing day was torture.

Sure, I could have him, but only if I wanted to commit to dating.

I didn't date.

I had a very valid reason for that.

Staying away from relationships had served me well over the years. My heart was in a good position, completely intact—aside from the heartache of my mother abandoning me—and I didn't have to worry about breakups or losing another person I loved.

But when I looked into those grayish-green eyes across the table from me, my valid reasons packed up and hightailed it out of there. My heart got googly eyes and pshawed any excuse I'd ever had about avoiding relationships. And my dick panted like a damn dog in heat.

Lance Ingram was a potent drug and I was the junkie right there waiting for a hit—knowing it was a bad idea, knowing it could fuck things up beyond belief, but not caring because all I wanted to do was feed that incessant need clawing in my gut. The need to touch him, to be close to him, to be the reason for his smile.

A lady who'd been working for Henry for years brought out our tray of food and placed plates in front of us. Once she'd deposited napkins and ketchup, she left us with instructions to wave her down if we needed anything.

Lance chuckled and pointed at my plate. "Doesn't look like grilled lemon pepper chicken or sautéed vegetables."

"Damn it, they forgot my sparkling water too," I joked.

My *usual* on a weekday consisted of a tenderloin and onion rings. Weekends, I'd usually opt for a burger or chicken sandwich with fries. The roadhouse did a mean steak and baked potato one Sunday a month, and salmon and veggies straight from the grill another Sunday each month, but for the most part, they stuck to tried-and-true bar food. The fancier fare always did well and brought in good money, but not enough to abandon the regular menu items.

Henry had pretty much perfected the specials rotation to match up best with which sporting events were taking place locally and nationally. And he had a wickedly keen sense of what folks in town or passing through wanted as each season came and went. He kept the menu traditional and only mixed things up when he knew it would be a good business decision.

"I just like to give Henry shit. He knows I'd rather have a tenderloin than grilled lemon pepper chicken," I said before taking a big bite of my sandwich.

Lance started in on his fries, dipping them in the cup of homemade ranch off to the side. He groaned. "Damn, there were a lot of things I missed about Haven Grove—a lot of reasons I'm glad to be back for good—but this fucking ranch is hands down the best in all the world."

I smirked. "How about a t-shirt with *The Best Damn Ranch in All the Land* for the roadhouse?"

He smiled, bringing a napkin to his mouth to wipe away the smudge of ranch I'd already thought about licking away at least five times. "I like it. See? I knew you'd have some good ideas—just needed to give you enough time to mull it over."

We continued to chat easily as we ate dinner. Several customers came and went, the locals saying hi to folks they knew, the travelers just stopping by seeming to take stock and quickly judge the roadhouse as a friendly place.

When a man walked into the bar with a black and white striped shirt, I couldn't help the memory and laughter from bubbling up.

"What?" Lance asked.

"Just thinking about something," I said, shoving a fry in my mouth.

Lance narrowed his eyes and waited.

I huffed. "See the guy up by the bar with the black and white striped shirt?" Lance nodded and I continued. "Well, when I was about twenty-two, I met up with this guy—"

"You were doing the no-dating-random-hookup thing all the way back then?" Lance interrupted.

"Duh, you just hadn't figured yourself out or noticed this fine ass yet," I teased.

Lance shook his head as if trying to clear the fog. "I didn't know..." he muttered. "Wasn't even on my radar..." He blew out a breath. "Damn clueless."

I wasn't sure if his little monologue was regarding me, hookup apps, his sexuality, or what, so I left him with his thoughts and went on. "Anyway, I'd picked out this black and white striped shirt to wear—"

Lance's eyes bored into mine. "Thought you didn't date?"

Rolling my eyes with a huff, I said, "Wasn't a *date*, I

was meeting up with him. Had to wear clothes of some sort. Now, will you let me tell my story?"

His face softened and he smiled. "Sorry, yeah. Tell your story." His words were gentle and encouraging.

For a second, my chest got all fluttery and tight. I took a long gulp of water, wondering if I'd not been hydrating enough. "*Anyway*, I have on this black and white striped shirt and I get to the bar where I'm meeting this guy. He buys me a drink and we're kinda bopping along to the music—I'm trying to figure out how to move things along and get us to the good part of the night. He leans in and says, 'You look really hot tonight.' I mean, I'm young and horny so the words go straight to my dick. I try to look all sexy and shit—"

"Try?" Lance scoffed. "Like it takes a lot..."

Heat zinged through me. "So, I sip my drink and say all sultry-like, 'Just call me jailbait.' He nearly chokes on his drink and gives me a weird look. 'How old are you?' he asks. I'm not sure where the question came from, but I'm all about getting laid, so I shrug and say, 'Old enough.' This guy eyes me up and down and makes some excuse about a migraine coming on. Hightails it out of there. I ended up going home with some other dude, but I was confused for years about why the first guy left."

Lance, listening intently, frowned. "I don't get it, why did you tell him to call you jailbait? You know he left because he thought you were underage, right?"

I laughed again, at the memory and Lance. "Yeah, well, my dumb ass didn't realize until a few years later that 'jailbait' referred to an underaged person. *I* thought people said jailbait when someone was wearing black and white stripes—you know, like a prisoner?"

Lance blinked slowly and then busted out laughing. He laughed until he cried and I just ate my dinner as this beautiful silver fox daddy I'd known since birth wiped tears from his eyes. "Oh god, that's amazing."

I smirked. "I can laugh about it now. At the time, I felt like a moron."

Dinner continued with conversation about the peach trees, the store stock I needed to unload, and the Sweet & Creamy getting ready to reopen. Occasionally, Lance would snort with laughter, and when the guy in the black and white striped shirt walked by, he nearly choked on a fry when he got all giggly again.

I loved every single moment of it.

Once our plates were cleared, Lance pulled his notebook in front of him. "Okay, whatcha got?"

Henry kept the peach-inspired mixed drinks coming while Lance and I dove head-first into planning for world domination between an orchard, a general store, an ice cream shop, and a roadhouse.

I hadn't laughed so much in years. Honestly, aside from laughing with my brother, I probably hadn't laughed that much in my entire life.

By the time the "business meeting" ended, we had a plan.

It was a really great plan, even if I did say so myself, and I found myself excited about the prospect of bringing the Juicy Peach and the store back to the height of their glory days.

We planned to approach a local business with what we

needed as far as t-shirts. If Francie could take on our order and keep us stocked, Lance and I both preferred giving our business to local folks. If not, we'd look to the guy Lance knew back in the city.

For the bumper stickers, water bottle and laptop decals, magnets, and stickers, I suggested a husband and wife in Haven Grove who were about a year into their Etsy shop adventure. I'd seen their work and I thought they'd likely be able to help us produce exactly what we wanted. And if what we needed was too much, Lance's guy was set up for bigger orders.

But staying local was a definite plus for both of us.

Henry suggested a lady just outside of Haven Grove who could probably do what we wanted with coffee cups, shot glasses, tumblers, water bottles, and beer mugs. He'd given us her contact information and we already had a phone call in to her to set up a meeting.

Lance was going to talk to his guy back in the city about getting the gift cards designed and printed. Each card could be purchased at any of the four locations, loaded with funds from our shared website—which was something Lance had a guy working on the moment he got the okay from Henry and me—and the money on the gift card could be spent at any of the four businesses. I didn't completely understand the technical side of it, but Lance had explained that the web designer would set things up so each business kept its own website, but they were tied together as far as the gift card transactions and whatnot.

Word of mouth would be the best way to let people know they could get a five percent discount on any purchase at the four businesses if they had a purchase receipt within ten days from one of the other places. However, we had Lance's guy working on four signs to put at the registers and a stack of flyers to post around town.

All of the merchandise we'd discussed getting made would come in two categories. First, each item would be available with our tried-and-true logos. We were going to work with the local guy who originally made the logos for the roadhouse, the orchard, the store, and the ice cream shop to have him brush them up just a bit before we slapped them on merchandise.

The second category included the funny and or slightly suggestive phrases available on each item. Lance and I had nearly laughed ourselves silly coming up with ideas, but we'd finally decided on a top ten—with a handful of them being used first to see how things went, and adding the others to the stock as demand allowed.

Opting to use the shortened form of Dairy Palace as DP for the mileage we hoped to get with the innuendo, we'd settled on:

I Rode Hard at Riggs' Roadhouse

Love That Juicy Peach

I Love Sweet & Creamy DP

The Best Damn Ranch in ALL the Land – The Riggs Family Roadhouse

I Want My Juicy Peach Sweet & Creamy

My Juicy Peach Loves It Sweet & Creamy

DP'd at the Sweet & Creamy

DP My Juicy Peach

My Juicy Peach Got DP'd and Rode Hard at Riggs' Roadhouse

Sweet & Creamy – The Only Way I Want My Juicy Peach DP'd

Lance could have likely done most of the work himself. Hell, I could have probably pulled off most of the work even while being swamped with the orchard and store. Instead, my stupid ass suggested we have a standing dinner meeting—whether at the roadhouse or one of our places—or at least a phone call every day so we stayed in contact about what was taken care of, what our next steps were, and if we'd run into any trouble along the way.

I didn't really expect any business issues, but my dick was hoping to get into all sorts of trouble with Lance.

If you're not careful, your damn heart's gonna get involved in that mess.

Nah, Lance knew where I stood.

I'd made it all these years without allowing my heart to get broken again. One guy wasn't going to change that.

Even if that one guy was the sexiest fucking silver fox I'd ever seen.

"It's good to have him home," Henry said quietly later that night while I stared out the window washing dishes at closing time.

His words jerked me from my trance. "Huh? Who?"

Henry smirked and gave me a knowing look. "Playin' it that way, huh?" When my face flamed, he chuckled. "Couldn't do much better than Lance," he said.

Scrunching up my face, I scoffed. "He's Dad's age," I argued weakly. "Plus, I don't *do* relationships—better than or worse than."

Henry pursed his lips as if thinking. "Lance seems to be the type who wants more than just fooling around."

"Yeah," I said on a regretful sigh about two seconds before I realized I'd given myself away. "Not that I'd do anything with him, serious or casual."

Henry didn't buy it based on the way he laughed. "Hudson, I'm not your gatekeeper. You've made it this far being true to yourself, I'm not going to try to change that." He grabbed a glass and rubbed it dry. "I don't know what's best, I'm just saying I haven't seen that look on your face...well, *ever*. If he can make you smile that way, I'm on Team Lance."

Allowing his words to sink in, I narrowed my eyes. "You'd support me getting involved with a guy twenty years older than me? A guy who has known me since birth? You'd cheer me on if I said I wanted Dad's best friend to fuck my brains out?"

Henry slapped me with a towel. "Don't be a shit. Twenty years shouldn't matter. I think this is one of those situations where *age is just a number* comes into play. I might have balked before, but seeing you two sitting out there tonight, I don't see the age thing being a problem.

"As far as Lance knowing us since birth, that's just weak. He knew us since birth because he's Dad's best friend. He was as much a Riggs way back then as we were. He's always been like family and we were lucky to have him as a role model as we grew up," Henry said.

"Okay, how's it weak? You don't think people are going to wonder if anything inappropriate was going on way back when?"

Henry snorted. "First, since when do you worry about

what people think? Second, anyone who knows Lance—back then, now, or both—knows in the depths of their soul that he would rather gouge his eyes out than do something inappropriate or harmful to anyone, let alone a kid."

My brother was right.

"And the part about him being Dad's best friend? Don't you think that's going to get a little weird?" I asked.

Henry cleared his throat. "Ah, um, yeah. *That* part might get a bit dicey."

I huffed out a breath. "*Dicey*. Yeah. Like Dad might dice us both to pieces."

"I think you can see where things go before letting Dad know anything."

Realizing too late where I'd let the conversation go, I shook my head, doing my best to clear out the hopeful vibes. "Won't matter. If I get my way, we'll have something quick and easy—I may even let it go on longer than my usual one-time thing—then we'll move on with our lives. Dad wouldn't ever have to know." I gave my brother a look.

Henry held up a hand. "Dad won't hear it from me. But anyone with eyes can see that you and Lance are hot for each other, so don't be surprised if rumors fly. Personally, I don't see how you could get involved with him and then move on like nothing happened when you'll see him daily. Don't know how either of you could watch the other get involved with someone else, but maybe that's just me and my hang-ups when it comes to relationships."

The thought of Lance with someone else was an icy

hand gripping my balls. *Oh, hell no* was the first thing that ran through my head.

But I shook the thought away.

I'd hooked up with a couple guys I still saw quite often. I knew they'd gone on to fuck other people. One was married with kids now. Two guys I'd messed around with were now engaged. One guy had just sent me an open house invitation to see the home he'd bought with his new husband.

None of that bothered me in the least.

Why?

Because that was how I liked it. We'd hooked up, things had been good, and we'd moved on. No hard feelings, no *feelings* at all.

Then why does the thought of Lance with someone else have you feeling downright shitty and ready to eat nails?

As if reading my mind, Henry's smirk reappeared. "You been doing much hooking-up since Lance came back to town? Many massages?"

I sneered at him. "Been a bit busy," I bit out.

He just nodded, his eyes sparkling.

"What? I have," I said, doing my best not to sound like a whining little brother.

Henry shrugged. "Didn't say anything."

I yanked the plug on the sink to let the water drain. "Didn't have to," I muttered. "Can see it in your eyes. I've been *busy*. Period. Doesn't have anything to do with Lance."

"'Course not," Henry drawled. "Thanks for helping." He gathered up towels and headed toward the laundry room shared by the roadhouse and the apartment Henry occupied. Stopping, he turned back to me. "Just know it's okay to let yourself be happy if you find someone worth letting your guard down for."

I studied my brother for a brief moment before nodding. "Could stand to take your own advice, ya know?"

Henry smiled. "Yeah, well, we're talking about you, not me."

My brother walked away, and I wondered if either of us would ever be able to heal enough from our mom leaving to find happiness.

Maybe you just need to find someone worth letting your guard down for. An echo of Henry's words teased at the back of my mind.

My phone buzzed with a text from Lance.

Lance: Love the shit we got planned. Glad to be doing this with you. Sleep tight.

I reacted to his words with a thumbs-up emoji.

But I smiled all the damn way home.

Chapter 6
Lance

I was screwed.

Exhausted.

And screwed.

How I ever thought I could work day in and day out with Hudson and not be in a heap of trouble, I'd never know. But there I was, seeing him daily. Basking in the glow of his smile. Swooning when it was *me* who made him laugh. Soaking up everything that made him Hudson.

Hudson.

The man I was no longer infatuated and falling for…I'd done gone right ahead and dove head first into being all the way gone for him.

I'd been home nearly two months.

The Sweet & Creamy was up and running again, bringing in more business and revenue than it had at the same time last year according to our financial records.

Hudson and I met or spoke nearly every day and our business relationship worked like a well-oiled machine.

I'd slotted right back into the Riggs family since coming home, almost as if I'd never left. Casey Joe and I met up for lunch every week, and Henry never failed to offer a listening ear or a friendly smile.

Hudson reported the peach trees had bloomed even better than he'd hoped in the spring and the fruit would be coming on soon. The orchard was bringing in slightly more money at a slow time of the year than it had for the last few years if the books were to be believed.

The general store was hoppin', and I knew a lot of it had to do with us combining forces. Even Henry reported a spike in business recently.

All of that was amazing.

Perfect.

Exactly what we'd wanted.

I didn't mind the hard work, especially when we saw such great returns.

But I was about to lose my fucking mind over Hudson.

My attraction to him had never been *just* physical, but it had swiftly warped into something a lot deeper and more meaningful than thinking he was hot.

I knew without a doubt that Hudson was attracted to me in return.

Yet, we somehow managed to work together pretty much daily and not be affected by the strong pull between us.

Maybe because he'd had years of keeping people at a distance.

Maybe because the fear of losing someone like he did when Missy walked away was strong enough to override the attraction.

Whatever his secret, I didn't have the same abilities and I was going absolutely bat-shit with how badly I wanted him.

Wanted to kiss him, touch him, yeah. But more than that, I wanted to take him on a date. Do nice things for him. Hold him in my arms while he slept. Make a picnic lunch and take him on a long drive while we chatted about nonsense as the clouds floated by.

Instead, I got to see him almost daily and had to pretend my heart wasn't about to pound out of my chest.

It was the worst.

But also the best.

Everything was better when Hudson and I were together.

Sure, I'd had to accept the eternal blue balls.

And my breathing always felt a little off when he was around.

But I could live with those things if it meant having him near me.

The problem was, I just couldn't stop wanting more.

Hudson had told me to stop by his place for lunch one day. He wanted to show me some things he'd done with the Juicy Peach and general store.

I'd always loved the Riggs' farmhouse and seeing Hudson making it his own did something funny inside my chest. He was a small-town farm boy through and through, and he absolutely glowed in his element. Taking over the orchard and store may have been a huge load in the beginning, but Hudson was damn smart—and hella tenacious—and he'd gone and got the whole thing working better in just over six months than Billy had done in a lifetime of running the place.

"Nice cock," I deadpanned as Hudson and I cleared the remnants of our lunch from his kitchen table.

Hudson's eyes shot wide as he glanced at me over his shoulder.

"The rooster? On the clock?" I pretended innocence as I pointed at the wall clock.

His cheeks pinked slightly. "Oh, yeah, I found a few rooster items at a flea market. Thought it fit the farmhouse vibe."

We made our way toward the Juicy Peach, talking easily on the warm summer day. The Riggs family took up a large chunk of Haven Grove with Casey Joe in one of the farmhouses, Henry living in the apartment above the roadhouse, and Hudson in the orchard farmhouse.

The orchard itself spread over a few acres of land to the west and north of Hudson's place. The public pretty much never saw the farther corners of the orchard—the *you pick* sections rotated through the portions closer to the Juicy Peach general store. A portable checkout stand moved as needed to supply you-pickers with different sizes of bags and baskets, and to check them out when they'd filled their bags. The *you pick* business had always been cash-only, but Hudson had opted to upgrade internet and add a hotspot to the check-out stand so folks wanting to pay with a card would be able once picking season arrived.

"It's not much," Hudson was saying as we walked toward the backdoor of the Juicy Peach general store. "I just wanted to spruce things up a bit. Had a couple of the kids do a thorough sweep and wash things down before we restocked earlier in the week." He opened the door and waited for me to walk past. "Just thought you could let me know if it's too much—don't wanna look cheesy—or if it fits the small-town peach orchard and general store vibe."

I'd spent the day moping when Hudson had taken a trip to an auction and flea market a couple towns over. He'd asked me to go, but I'd had to say no. Mainly, because I didn't have anyone to work the shop that day. Only somewhat because I wasn't sure I could spend an entire day with him without exploding.

But he'd come back all smiles with his new purchases and I'd kicked myself for not figuring out a way to take the road trip with him.

He'd added a few touches to the store. The place had always had an authentic feel with its worn wood floors and handmade wooden shelves. The whole interior was wood, rope, and antiques—many of the items from way back when the Riggs family started their orchard and store.

The double doors upfront rang an old-fashioned bell when anyone entered. Off to the left was a long counter and antique cash register. General groceries and supplies lined shelves in rows up and down the middle of the store. Over to the right was the bakery counter with a small row of five swivel stools for the occasional customer to take a seat and enjoy a treat.

Hudson had added a gigantic piece of artwork on the main wall, directly in the middle at the back where every eye would land on it. A four-foot tin peach with a huge rooster—when I say huge, I mean five feet of painted tin, beak, crow, hackle, and all—posing next to the fruit.

A few more antique pieces boasting peaches and roosters were tastefully displayed around the shop. Right behind the cash register sat a large 3D peach with a three-foot-tall rooster, complete with twinkly lights, standing next to it.

"I get the peaches, but what's with the roosters?" I asked.

Hudson smirked and shrugged. "I've got a thing for cocks."

And with that, my brain short-circuited, and I was done.

Over and out.

Finished.

I sighed as I eased myself down onto my bed. I'd painted a wall in the shop after closing time the night before, and my muscles were absolutely screaming. I'd spent the day swallowing acetaminophen and trying to stay active so my muscles wouldn't stiffen up, but I'd finally let the two teens at the shop promise they'd close up and dragged myself home for a hot bath in Epsom salts.

Feeling like the oldest of old men, I reached for my phone and searched for massage *places* near me. When the closest location was over twenty miles away, I searched for massage *services* near me. That got a few more hits. After scrolling, I found a comment on a site regarding a massage provider who would bring a table to your home or place of business and perform thirty-, sixty-, or ninety-minute massages.

Bingo.

I clicked the link the commenter provided and ended up on a business directory-type page. Clicking the only entry that appeared to have anything to do with massage, I found myself staring at a very simple service and price page.

Name. Easy enough.

Address. I typed in the apartment address and put a note to have the provider come to the back entrance so as not to disrupt business. Plus, I didn't need everyone and their brother in Haven Grove knowing I was so old I needed a massage after painting a wall.

After choosing my day and time, I moved on to the drop-down menus for length of massage and services.

Thirty, sixty, or ninety minutes?

Ninety. Bring it on.

Type of massage? Swedish or deep-tissue?

Swedish. I needed a soft touch and relaxing, nothing digging into my muscles for the time being.

Services? Spot focus? Full-body? Full service*?

Hell, why not? Go big or go home. As sore as I was, I wanted everything and the kitchen sink. Hopefully *full service* would have me able to move without crying.

I paid the fifty-percent up-front fee, included my phone number, scrolled quickly through the legal gobbly-gook, checked the consent box, and submitted the appointment request.

Dreaming of a mid-morning massage to ease my pain, I took more acetaminophen and hoped for a restful night.

Morning came and I found the pain slightly better, but my joints and muscles had seized up like the Tin Man.

Glancing at the clock, knowing I wasn't scheduled for the Sweet & Creamy until late afternoon, I rolled from bed to start coffee and drag myself to the shower before my traveling massage arrived.

Morning me was grateful that nighttime me had made the massage for ten o'clock. That gave me time to opt out of the shower and run another bath to soak in. Plus, I'd have about two hours to enjoy my coffee, check the news, tidy up a few business tasks, and just enjoy the morning.

Doing my best *not* to imagine what it would be like to start each day with Hudson by my side, I dried off, threw on a pair of joggers, and padded to the kitchen to pour my first cup of coffee. Below the apartment, the ice cream shop was silent for the moment. Jan, the middle-aged woman who'd been working at the Sweet & Creamy for years, would arrive in about ninety minutes to start the process of opening.

With my mind still mostly on Hudson, no matter how hard I tried, I allowed myself a moment to think of the conversation we'd had about possibly adding in a couple simple soups and sandwiches to the menu at lunch and dinner time.

My first thought had been I didn't want to take business from the roadhouse. But Hudson, and later Henry, had made a valid point that most people who would be stopping in for ice cream wouldn't be ones heading to the roadhouse after. If anything, the roadhouse lunch or dinner people might stop by for ice cream, but they wouldn't be stopping in for ice cream on their way to eat at the bar. So, having a couple other menu items might make sense—financially speaking. I'd just have to make sure the soups and sandwiches were easy to make and wouldn't put a kink in our flow.

I started a second cup of coffee while balancing a couple expenses in the books. As usual, my mind drifted back to Hudson. I hadn't thought about him as much in the twenty-five years I knew him before I left town, but now, every second of every day seemed to have some form of Hudson-sized thoughts bombarding my brain.

I knew Hudson had been busy lately. I knew that was likely the only reason I hadn't had to accept the fact he was going out to hook up with random guys. Between the orchard, the store, the bar, the odd jobs he did around town, and helping me with peaches and cream domination, the guy had pretty much zero downtime. And if he did have a moment to breathe, he seemed hell-bent on filling the time with something productive. I wasn't sure if he knew how to relax.

Eventually, he's going to get into a routine and go back to his hookups.

Hating the thought, I poured a third cup of coffee. I wasn't exactly sure that hyping myself on caffeine before I was supposed to relax during a massage was the best idea, but what was done was done.

What if I just accepted the offered hookup with Hudson?

Would I be able to keep him coming back for more?

Could I survive the inevitable when he finally cut me off?

Would the friendship be strong enough to make it through something like that?

Would my *heart* survive?

What was my other option? Stay locked in the standstill with Hudson's stubborn ass and be miserable wanting what I couldn't have.

As I drained the last of the coffee and rinsed the mug, I stared out the kitchen window. Looking over Haven Grove, knowing I'd spend the rest of my days in the town I called home, I ran through my choices.

One, I could continue with the way things were. Refusing anything with Hudson because he wasn't willing to go further than casual. Going this route meant blue-ball frustration, pining and longing, the gut-punch of watching Hudson go about his life with other guys, and plastering a smile on my face to hide how badly I wanted the man.

Not the best option, but fairly safe. Painful, frustrating, and slightly less than mediocre, but safe.

Mostly.

Two, I could give in and do the one-time thing with Hudson.

This option had subsections.

Subsection A was that we went through with the hookup, it was good but not as mind-blowing as we'd hoped, and everything returned to normal pretty quickly.

Subsection B was we went through with the hookup, it was mind-blowing, we agreed to keep things going—casually, of course—until we both decided to move on and go back to just being business partners and family friends.

Subsection C was we went through with the hookup, it was mind-blowing as we'd predicted, Hudson realizes all he's been missing out on, he declares his love for me, and we live happily ever after.

Now, each of these subsections also had a .1 side note.

That side note was pretty much the same for A, B, and C, just changing slightly on each for the sake of creativity.

A.1- Casey Joe finds out his best friend fucked his son. Casey Joe castrates his best friend.

B.1- Casey Joe discovers best friend and son together, drowns best friend in a vat of peach vodka.

C.1- Casey Joe hears about his best friend and son being together, runs best friend out of town with a pitch fork and flaming torch.

A side note to the side note was that any .1 could be attached to any subsection at any time.

Running my hands over my face, I groaned.

I wanted C—preferably without the .1—but I knew it was stupid and assumptive to think sex with me would just magically make Hudson change his mind about relationships.

Maybe option B is best. You both get what you want, at least for a short time, and you can win him over during the time you're keeping things casual.

Huffing out a breath, I bent at the elbows, leaning heavily against the sink, and dropped my head into my hands. My muscles protested the position, but I didn't care. Part of me wanted to be just as stubborn as Hudson and hold out. He knew I wanted more. Why should I be the one to bend?

On the other hand, who was I really punishing if I let the stalemate continue?

Hell, at this point, maybe the offer of casual sex wasn't even on the table any longer. Running a hand through my hair, I closed my eyes. I was too damn old for this shit.

Grumbling as I pushed away from the sink, I checked

the time. My free morning had done nothing to really clear my head, but at least I could relax for ninety minutes. Maybe the massage would give me time to evaluate the situation yet again and come to a conclusion.

And, if not, at least I had an hour and a half of endorphin-releasing relaxation to look forward to.

A knock sounded and pulled me from my head.

Glancing at the living room with a brief moment of worry that the room wasn't big enough for a whole massage table, I walked toward the door.

Pulling the door open, only briefly wondering if I should have put on a shirt, I smiled as I prepared to meet my massage provider.

Confusion rocketed through me at the pink-cheeked, smirking Hudson standing before me.

With a quick glance at the large folded table gripped by a handle in his right hand, I brought my eyes back to meet his sparkling blue ones. Like a slow-moving glacier, my brain finally caught up.

"You've got to be kidding me," I muttered.

"You ordered a massage?"

"Is there any job you *don't* do?"

"What can I say? I'm a jack of all trades," Hudson said, shouldering his way through the door. Maneuvering the table, he leaned it against the couch. "So, you signed up for ninety minutes of *full*-service massage. Let's just get the paperwork out of the way and we'll get started."

"Why'd you say it like that?" I asked, narrowing my eyes.

"Like what?" Hudson blinked innocently. I was suddenly reminded of the time I caught him sneaking cookies from the jar Billy kept in the back room at the store.

"*Full* service," I repeated the words with emphasis on the word full.

"Well, the option you chose includes...um, well, it means we both enjoy the massage and things end on a very...um, *happy* note."

"What the fuck are you—" Even as the words spilled from my mouth, understanding smacked me in the face. Pinching the bridge of my nose, I chuckled humorously. "Fuuuuuck."

Chapter 7
Hudson

THE APPOINTMENT NOTIFICATION HAD COME IN the night before just as I'd gotten out of the shower. My run had gone well and a round of weights at the gym had my arms feeling like noodles. When I'd finally gotten home, all I'd wanted to do was wash off the sweat and head to bed.

The summer night air drifted through the windows, teasing my nose with the scent of the last sweet peach blossoms as I settled into bed. My phone buzzed and I clicked the notification.

Most of my massages came from a couple of the hookup apps. Guys would see I was nearby, see in my profile that I offered full-service massages, and hit me up. Only a few of my appointments ever came from the local business directory, but the listing was free so there was no reason *not* to advertise there.

Money was money.

Whether eighty dollars an hour for your run-of-the-mill one-hour massage or one-twenty an hour for a *full-service* massage, the work was easy enough—and often pretty damn enjoyable—plus, I liked staying busy and helping people feel good.

Reading through the appointment request, and then reading through it again, I laughed out loud.

Holy.

Fucking.

Shit.

Lance had requested a massage.

A full-service, ninety-minute massage.

He'd signed up for ten o'clock in the morning, paid the fifty-percent up-front fee, and signed the consent.

Obviously, he hadn't known it was *me* he was requesting to run my hands all over him. And he definitely didn't read the consent form thoroughly or he would have very likely realized what he was signing up for.

Like the evil Kermit meme, I sat in bed propped against the headboard, one part of me saying, *Tell him and save him the awkwardness*, while the other part of me demanded, *Give that man the best orgasm of his life and see if he can keep stonewalling you.*

Shit.

I didn't want to put Lance in an awkward position.

But...

I grinned to myself as I thought about showing up at his place with my table.

Fuck it.

He'd signed up for ninety minutes of full service and that was exactly what he was going to get.

That is, if he still wanted it once he saw it was me and realized what he'd signed up for.

A thought struck me. Maybe he *did* realize what the full-service massage was. A zing of jealousy traveled through me at the thought of Lance getting off with anyone else.

And what exactly do you think is going to happen if you keep pushing him into the casual-fuck-slash-friend-zone? He's eventually going to find someone else to spend time with.

My stomach soured.

Nope.

Lance was getting the full-service treatment, and we'd deal with the consequences later.

Which was how I found myself at Lance's door a couple minutes before ten o'clock. I wasn't one hundred percent sure how it was all going to go down, but my body hummed with anticipation. Obviously, I wasn't going to force the guy to do something he didn't want to do, but I also wasn't going to turn down the chance to get off with him if he wanted to follow through with what he'd signed up for.

The look on Lance's face when he realized *I* was the massage provider was absolutely priceless.

"You ordered a massage?" I asked, doing my best to keep the glee from my words.

"Is there any job you *don't* do?" Lance grumbled.

"What can I say? I'm a jack of all trades." I shouldered my way through the door. Maneuvering the table, I leaned it against the couch. "So, you signed up for ninety minutes of *full*-service massage. Let's just get the paperwork out of the way and we'll get started."

"Why'd you say it like that?" Lance asked, narrowing his eyes.

"Like what?" I blinked, trying to look nonchalant and innocent. I was suddenly reminded of the time Lance caught me sneaking cookies from the jar Billy kept in the back room at the store.

"*Full* service," Lance repeated the words with emphasis on the word full.

"Well, the option you chose includes…um, well, it means we both enjoy the massage and things end on a very…um, *happy* note," I explained.

"What the fuck are you—"

I saw the moment understanding smacked Lance in the face.

Pinching the bridge of his nose, Lance chuckled humorously. "Fuuuuuck."

Pulling the paperwork from my bag, I moved toward the table in Lance's little apartment. The place wasn't fancy or huge, but it was tidy and had plenty of room for one person. He hadn't changed it much from when his mom lived there, but I noticed he'd removed a lot of the more frilly and tacky décor she'd been drawn to.

"So, we'll discuss what we're comfortable with upfront. If, at any point during the massage, you choose to keep things non-sexual, you just say the word. I'll check in from time to time to make sure you're comfortable with the pacing, pressure, and taking things further." I added our names to the paperwork and dated it. "I don't have an appointment after this, so we're good to let things take a bit longer."

The look on Lance's face told me he hadn't completely

come to terms with things. "I just wanted a damn massage because I overdid it painting," he muttered. "I didn't know *you* would be giving the massage, and I most definitely didn't mean to solicit a sexual service." He ran a hand over his face. "Fucking hell."

My heart sank a bit, but I wouldn't press him to do something he didn't want to do. "No worries, we can still do the regular massage. I'm certified, so I can definitely help with the sore muscles." I tapped the pen against the paper. "We can just sign here and get started."

"What do I have to sign if you're just doing a plain ol' massage?" Lance asked, his brow furrowed as he glanced at the paper.

"This part of meeting a new client is always a bit awkward. If they signed up for regular, we just go with regular and I don't even mention the other options. If they signed up for *full* service, I have to confirm they knew what they were signing up for. Some guys are like, *Yes, definitely. Totally knew what I was signing up for. Let's get started.* But a lot of guys are either on the fence, not sure if they want to follow through, or don't really know what they want." I pressed my finger to the paperwork. "That's where this comes in. We discuss our do's and don'ts. We decide on a plan. Then we get started and see where things go. The client controls the situation—at least to a certain degree, it's not like I just agree to anything they want to do—and I almost always leave a very satisfied client. Whether because the massage was just that great or because they opted for something a bit more." I shrugged.

Lance looked from the papers to me and back to the

papers before pinching his nose. *"Almost always* leave a very satisfied client?"

Smirking, I nodded. "The ones who maybe aren't *as* satisfied usually end up scheduling another appointment and telling me they regretted not going with the full-service option." The scent of soap and coffee engulfed me, Lance's warm body so very close. I bumped my hip against his. "What other questions do you have? Maybe asking them will help you feel more comfortable."

He turned incredulous eyes my way. "I didn't make an appointment for sexual services," he growled.

I shrugged. "Okay, but I can still tell you have questions. Go ahead."

Lance looked a bit helpless for a few moments as if considering his next words. "Do things ever go wrong? You just open your table and fuck them right there? What about safety—of any type?"

"Never really had anything go wrong. There have been a handful of guys I'm just really not that into, so I only agree to the bare minimum hand job. If they're hot or I'm feeling some kind of way toward them, I'll usually sign off on blowjobs, one-sided or mutual." I twirled the pen between my fingers. "Only been a few guys I've let fuck me. That's not a part of the paperwork, so I discuss it with them beforehand and off-contract. I don't just open my table and let them fuck me. I do an actual massage. Most often, I'm pretty much just edging them for an hour or so and then I'm getting them off. I only get off if it's something we've agreed to beforehand. Safety is a must. Clients sign off on their health status if we're doing more than hand jobs. I'm careful and I take precautions to prevent anything unsafe."

"But what about the chance of meeting some creeper who wants to hurt you?" Lance asked, worry etched on his face.

My heart lurched, loving the fact he cared so much.

"It's a risk, but it's never happened. I feel out the situation when I arrive. If the vibe were to be bad, I'd leave.

Lance furrowed his brow. "I know you're a grown man, but I can't say I like the idea of you putting yourself in a situation that could be dangerous."

Smiling softly, I bumped into him again. "That's sweet and it's appreciated." A weird flutter lit up my stomach at the thought of Lance being concerned about me. Aside from Dad and Henry—and Billy, somewhat—I'd never really dealt with someone worrying about me.

Missy sure as hell didn't.

But the fact Lance was concerned for my safety had me feeling some sort of way. Honestly, I could have taken the route of being irritated that he was trying to control my life. But, in reality, I couldn't help the warm rush it gave me knowing Lance was worried about me.

"I really did just want a massage," he said sheepishly, rubbing the back of his neck.

"Do you want me to try my best to talk you into something a bit more than the regular massage?" I asked, my cheeks hot and my dick hopeful.

Lance glowered at me. "No." Then he sighed. "Yes?" He ran a hand through his gorgeous silver and black hair. "Fuck, Hudson, I don't know."

"Let's do the paperwork the way I'd usually do it with a client who is unsure," I suggested.

Lance nodded. "Yeah, fine."

We sat at the table and I willed my heartbeat to slow down and my breathing to steady.

"Before we get to the *other* part of the paperwork, let's start with the scents and oils. Any scents bother you? Allergic to scents or ingredients?"

Lance shook his head.

"I use a very light oil. I usually like to keep it unscented. I'll use essential oils in a diffuser. I brought a lavender candle, will that be okay?"

Lance nodded, his eyes darting to the paperwork.

Chuckling at his nervousness, I flipped the page.

"So, number one for me is no kissing," I said, pointing the pen at the line of words on the contract before I initialed.

"Why?" Lance asked, his scent doing delicious things to me, his face much too close to mine.

I shrugged. "Too personal. I don't kiss on hookups and I don't kiss during a massage."

"So, you've never kissed a guy?"

"I didn't say that," I said. "Just don't kiss people I'm not planning on taking things further with. So, I've not kissed *a lot* of guys."

"Guess we've got that in common," Lance said as he put his initials next to the no kissing clause.

The zing his words gave me almost had me doubling over. Thinking of Lance kissing someone sucked. Thinking of how good it would be for the two of us to share rare kisses lit a fire in my belly.

"These next ones will be things I check with you on. Even if you opt in here, you can opt out on the table." I tapped the pen on the paper. "Me giving you a hand job."

Lance bit his lip.

"You can say yes now and change your mind. You can always change your mind."

He nodded. "Okay, yeah." He initialed.

"You giving me a hand job."

Shaking his head, he opted out.

"Me giving you a blow job."

Lance initialed.

"You giving me a blow job."

He huffed. "I'm only saying no on these because I'm not sure I can keep feelings out of it."

"That's fine. Anything you opt into or out of is fine." I trailed the pen down the list. Part of me was disappointed that he didn't want to return the favor, but I understood his hesitation. The other part of me whispered that maybe it would be worth letting things tiptoe toward a relationship if it meant getting to experience some of these things *with* Lance rather than just doing them to him. "Assuming you opt into the full-service, do you want to get off?"

Lance nodded and added his initials.

"Are you okay with me getting off?"

The heat shading Lance's cheeks was adorable as he initialed his agreement.

Pointing the pen at the next line, I continued. "When was your last sexual health check-up? What were your results? And do you agree to sexually safe practices?"

Lance spoke as he filled in the information. "Right

before I left the city. Results have always been negative. And safe sex is good."

"I get tested regularly. Results are negative—I can show you if needed. And safe sex outside of a committed relationship is a must for me."

"Have you had a committed relationship?" Lance asked.

"Remember that guy I dated in high school? Tim? That's the closest I've had to a real relationship." I put a dot next to the final signature line. "Once we both sign here, we're good to go. I'll do a regular massage. At about the seventy-five minute mark, I'll check in with you regarding how you're feeling. At that point, we can finish the massage as usual, or I'll take things a bit further—depending on what you tell me."

"Okay," Lance said.

"Then the last step is paying the rest of the fee and we'll get started."

Lance pulled out his phone and tapped the screen. "Can I just send it straight to you or do I need to go back to the site?"

"Just send it to me," I said. We'd traded online payment information for the businesses, so I knew he already had my details.

Lance clicked a few times and my phone dinged. He shuffled a bit, gripping the back of his neck as he tossed his phone to couch. "Um, I've only had a few massages, how does this all work?"

"I'll set up the table while you go take off your clothes. You can use your own robe or the one I brought—it's completely clean, washed it myself in hot water and bleach. You'll come out here to a dimly lit room, some essential oils diffusing, a candle burning, and I'll head to the bathroom for a couple minutes until you call me out. You'll start on your stomach, robe off, blanket at your waist. The table isn't heated, so if you want a warm blanket, let me know and I'll ask to use your dryer for a moment."

"No, I'm good without the heat."

Resisting the completely foreign urge to lean in and kiss him, I stood abruptly. "Okay, sounds good. Let's get started." Ignoring how badly my body wanted to feel his mouth on mine, I walked toward my massage table. "Do you have a robe or want to borrow this one?"

Was it weird I wanted him to wear my robe so I could ball it up and sleep with it every night?

Yeah, that was fuckin' weird. But Lance had me completely out of my comfort zone and, apparently, I turned into a creeper when I was knocked off my game.

"I have a robe."

"Okay, just take your time. Come out when you're ready."

About ten minutes later, I had the bed set up, the oils diffusing, the candle lit, and Lance's living room lights dimmed.

Lance walked into the room, backlit by the bathroom light.

Fuck.

I was in over my head for sure.

Clearing my throat, I gestured toward the table. "Get comfortable. Holler at me when you're ready." I tried not to breathe in his scent when he passed me as I headed to the bathroom.

Washing my hands, splashing some water on my face, and taking deep breaths while looking out the tiny window overlooking Haven Grove, I calmed myself.

Well, I calmed myself the best I could.

Never in all of my hookups or massages had I been so amped up.

What the hell was it with Lance that heightened absolutely everything?

Recalling my childhood with him around, we'd always been close. He'd take Henry and me on drives, letting us take turns driving when we were old enough to reach the pedals. Lance often persuaded Dad to let us stay up just a bit later when there was something we wanted to watch. He was always the first to join in whatever outside game my brother and I were playing—maybe not having kids of his own made him more apt to play since he wasn't parenting. Or maybe Dad just didn't have the energy after everything with Missy and Billy.

But Lance had been a constant in my life.

Until he left.

And here I was, stuck between a rock and a hard place.

Fighting new desires and old demons.

With no ability to predict the outcome, only trauma of the past to guide my thinking, I needed to either stick to my guns or step out with faith.

Refuse to budge—casual sex or nothing—or take a chance and see where things could go.

Where things might go? Right back to the city, out of your life. Nobody stays.

"If I don't stay, they can't leave," I mumbled to myself. Taking a deep, fortifying breath, I renewed my commitment to casual sex only. Protecting myself and sticking to my guns had worked for me since before Lance left town, and it would keep working for me now that he was back home.

"Ready," Lance called from the living room.

The apartment smelled of soft lavender and the combination essential oil I'd placed in the diffuser. Lance's broad shoulders and back lay before me on the table and everything I'd been thinking in the bathroom scurried out of my head.

Thumbing through my phone, I found the massage playlist I'd created and hit play. Dribbling a bit of oil on my hands, I rubbed them together. "I'm going to start on your back and shoulders." Lance's body tensed momentarily when I touched him, but the first few strokes relaxed him.

"Am I supposed to talk or stay quiet?" Lance asked, his words muffled by the bed's ring pillow.

Smiling as I focused on the muscles beneath my fingers, I said, "Whatever you're comfortable with. Some people talk the whole time. Some prefer to just enjoy the moment."

Lance appeared to be an *enjoy the moment* type guy because he settled into my touch and the only noises from him were soft grunts and groans as I worked on particularly stiff or sore parts of his body.

I moved from his shoulders to his head, a soft smile playing at my lips when he groaned. Many people loved having their head massaged.

I worked my way down his arms and took my time on his fingers, imagining his hands on me, our fingers entwined, how gentle and firm his touch would be.

"I'd like to work on your glutes if you're comfortable with that," I said softly.

Lance grunted, the sound at odds with the gentle, soothing tones of healing frequencies coming from my phone.

"I need words, please, Mr. Ingram," I teased.

"Yes, you can work on my glutes," Lance grumbled.

Positioning the blanket so only the body part I wanted to work on was exposed, I kept things professional as I went to work on the tight muscles in his ass.

His very *fine* ass.

Look, I was professional, but not fucking blind.

After attending to both sides of Lance's backside, I made my way down his legs. His calves seemed to be extra sore, likely from the ladder work while painting, so I worked on them a smidge longer.

Reaching his feet, a chuckle escaped me when Lance jerked and grunted. "You okay?"

"Fuck, that tickled."

"Sorry, should have warned you. Can I try again?"

"Yeah."

Lance wiggled and squirmed through it all, but he allowed me to work on his feet. By this time, we were approximately sixty minutes into the massage. "Go ahead and turn over," I directed, holding the blanket so he could maneuver himself to his back. "I'll work my way from your head and neck, down to your legs, and then you'll have the option of how you'd like things to end."

Lance remained quiet, his face like stone, eyes closed. Leaving his feet alone, I moved to the head of the bed and started in on his head. Massaging his scalp, his temples, his jaw, then working my hands under his head to the base of his skull and neck.

"Are you comfortable with me working on your pecs along with your shoulders and arms?" I asked.

Lance answered, "Yes." His words soft and relaxed.

I kept myself focused on the muscles as my hands glided over his broad chest, the crisp hair teasing my fingertips. I noticed Lance tense and grip the blanket gathered at his waist. "You good? Too much?"

"I'm good," he croaked.

"Tell me if anything isn't good for you. This is supposed to be relaxing, not something that causes distress."

I continued to work on his chest, shoulders, and arms. Then I shifted the blanket to work on his quads, the muscles tight either from his painting session or because Lance was anxious over what might come next.

Or both.

At the seventy-five minute mark, I spoke softly. "I can continue this. I can stop. Or I can do the full-service options we talked about. Your choice."

Lance was so quiet for so long, I feared he'd fallen asleep and didn't hear my question. Finally, words escaped on a strangled whisper, "I don't know."

"It's completely your choice," I said. "If you don't want—"

Lance laughed darkly. "It's definitely not because I

don't want," he growled. "It just feels...I don't even know how to describe it."

"Do you want my opinion?" I asked, keeping my words soft.

He grunted.

"I think this is an opportunity neither of us wants to turn down. If you're into it, let it happen. I definitely want to finish this the right way."

Lance grumbled something.

"I need words," I said.

"Stick with what we discussed," Lance said. "I want the full service."

Feeling like I'd just won the lottery, I wiped my hands on a towel. With other clients, if I planned on *only* a hand job, I'd keep things well-oiled. But with Lance, I had every intention of getting my mouth on him, and lavender oil wasn't my favorite flavor.

Shifting the blanket down to his knees, I found him hard and dripping, his pre-cum smearing against the salt and pepper hair of his lower abdomen. Thumbing over his slit, loving the hiss of pleasure escaping his lips, I took him in hand and stroked gently.

I kept my eyes glued to Lance's features as I stroked him. His chest rising and falling, his jaw clenched. He wanted this, but he didn't want to want it. Or, more likely, he wanted it, but he didn't want to want it the way it was being offered.

Bending to whisper at his ear, still stroking him gently, I said, "This may be all I can give, but I promise I can make it so good."

Lance turned his head, his mouth seeking, but I

shifted, giving him my cheek. We stayed that way for a moment, faces pressed together. Chests heaving, my fist stroking over his leaking shaft, both of us fighting for control of a situation that begged to burst into an inferno.

"Fine," Lance bit out. "I'll take what you can give. For now." A hand came up and gripped the back of my neck. "Just know, I'm as stubborn as you and I'm not giving up."

A shiver ran through me, his words—a threat or a promise?—setting me on fire. Shifting down his body, I teased a nipple with my tongue before making my way to his cock. "Can I suck you?" I asked.

Lance grunted.

"Words," I reminded, my voice silky hot.

"Suck me," Lance demanded.

Tonguing his slit, savoring the flavor, I twirled my tongue around his swollen cockhead before spreading my lips around him and taking him deep.

Lance cursed, his hips bucking. One hand fisted in my hair and guided my head, his hips thrusting gently as I cupped his balls.

I was hard and my body screamed for more as I bobbed up and down on his cock, spit and pre-cum mixing to make a mess of my lips and chin. We'd both finish in less than three minutes if I doubled down and worked Lance over.

But I wanted more.

If this was our one time, I wanted it to be more than a quick jerk and blow job. I popped off his cock, spit stringing between his dick and my chin.

Lance groaned and pushed up on his elbows. "What's wrong?"

"Want you inside me," I panted. "Please. I can't promise anything more than this. I know I'm fucked up, this is fucked up..." I paused, pressing a hand against my dick. "But...Lance. Please."

He was quiet for several heartbeats. I didn't *know* what he was thinking, but based on what my brain was doing, I had a pretty decent idea. While I was thinking about keeping things casual, Lance was likely planning ways to take things further. We were both probably thinking about how things didn't feel anywhere close to casual between us, but while I steeled myself to force it to be that way, Lance was probably grasping onto it with both hands, trying to figure out how to use this stupid, crazy connection to his advantage.

Taking hold of his dick again, I stroked softly. "Lance."

He swallowed, his Adam's apple bobbing, and brought his hands to his eyes. "If we do this, there's no going back to what we have now. We can say we'll try. Say things won't change." He huffed out a breath, rocking his hips slightly as I gently stroked him. "But things between us changed the moment I walked into that bakery and saw you sitting there. You can deny it all you want, but there's something here. I can be patient—for now."

"I can't—"

"We've got time," Lance interrupted. "And we've got something deeper than just old friends and business partners."

I wanted to argue. Wanted to tell him it wasn't fair that he wouldn't just take no for an answer and realize I wasn't cut out for anything *real*.

Instead, I took a deep breath and nodded. I could go

along with what he was saying if it meant getting what I wanted. "So..."

"What?"

"We didn't discuss this part," I said.

"Forget the damn paperwork," Lance growled.

Moving quickly to my bag I grabbed a condom. Returning to Lance's side, I refused to think about how badly I wanted to kiss him. How much I wanted him to lead me to his room and spend the day owning my body.

What the fuck was wrong with me lately?

Clearing my throat, I tore open the foil packet and rolled the latex down his shaft. "How do you want me?"

Lance chuckled with no humor. "Baby, if I had you the way I wanted you, I'd never let you go."

My heart clenched as unfamiliar emotions washed over me. *I'd never let you go.*

Oh, god.

I wanted to trust him. Wanted to believe his gruff, whispered words.

Shaking my head against the haze of lust and desire, I cleared my throat. "The table can hold us both," I hedged, smearing oil on his cock and my hole.

"This is your show, Hudson," Lance said, his words steely and controlled. "For now."

Trying to think of a slightly less intimate position, I crawled onto the table—forever grateful I'd splurged on the premium model—and straddled Lance's hips, my back turned toward his face.

If I had you the way I wanted you, I'd never let you go.

I couldn't catch my breath.

Ignoring the mini breakdown my head and heart

seemed to be smack dab in the middle of, I raised myself on my knees and guided his cock to my hole.

I wasn't going to lie. When I'd seen Lance's name on my appointments, I'd prepped and stretched in hopes of things turning into exactly this. As I sank down on him, his thick cockhead breaching my tight muscles, I groaned.

"Fuck, Lance," I bit out.

"You okay?" he asked, his big hands gripping my hips as he held himself still.

"Yeah, it's good. You're just thick."

He chuckled. "Never had any complaints, not that there's been many chances."

I lowered myself until I bottomed out and paused to take short, shallow breaths. "Fuck, just give me a second," I panted.

"I'm not going anywhere," Lance said, humor and promise lacing his words.

Losing myself in the rhythm, I rode him. Savoring the pleasure, the stretch of my body around him as each thrust brought his dick brushing over that sensitive bundle of nerves, sending shockwaves zinging through me.

Lance's hands were firm yet gentle as he gripped my hips. He touched me as if he thought I'd break, guiding me gently up and down his shaft. But his fingers gripped into my flesh from time to time as if fearful I'd disappear if he didn't hold on tight.

"Get off," Lance demanded. "I want you over the table."

The image of Lance taking me over the massage table set fire to my belly and had my balls drawing up tight. I shifted from the straddle and moved to the side of the table while Lance sat up and swung his legs over the side.

Pushing away the fact every cell in my body wanted to step between his thick thighs and wrap myself in his arms, I bent over the bed and spread my legs.

Lance muttered something about *crazy* and *think this is one time*, but he stepped behind me and slid his cock back into me. Like coming home, my body sang with pleasure to be filled by him. He set a hard and fast pace, and I suddenly hated every single man who'd been with him before me—was insanely jealous of anyone who would get to be with him after me.

It doesn't have to be that way.

I moaned, pushing myself back on his cock.

Increasing his speed, Lance bent over my back, wrapping his arms around my shoulders and chest. "Fuck, Hudson, I'm not gonna last. Can you come this way?"

"Yeah," I panted.

"Touch yourself."

Reaching for my rock-hard cock, I jerked myself in time to Lance's thrusting hips. Grunting, the tingle in my lower back telling me I was only seconds away, I stroked harder, focusing on the spectacular release my balls were about to have rather than the scent of Lance wrapped around me. His hard, hot breaths against my ear. Large hands cupping my shoulder and my hip.

Just as an orgasm ripped through me, Lance gave a final thrust and stilled, his cock pulsing deep in my body. With his chest plastered to my back, Lance grunted as he unloaded inside me, my body shaking with release as I shot all over his hardwood floor.

When we'd both come down from our high enough to catch our breaths, Lance pulled from my ass and stripped off the condom. Padding to the bathroom, he returned with two wet cloths and we cleaned up.

Anticipating a discussion I wasn't sure I was up for, I kept my back turned to him as I dressed. For the first time in my life, my usual disconnect and nonchalance with hookups was absent. I wanted to dash out of his apartment, but at the same time, I wanted to throw myself into his arms and let him make me promises.

Promises I wanted so damn badly to be true.

Everybody leaves.

Clearing my throat, I turned to face him. He'd dressed as well and his eyes were glued to the mess I'd made on his floor. Quickly, I used the wet cloth to wipe up the evidence of our time together. "I clean and sanitize all of my massage supplies," I said, feeling like an idiot.

"Good to know. I'll write it in the Yelp review."

"Are you..." I wasn't sure where that question was going. Was Lance good? Did he enjoy the massage? The sex? Was he mad at me? Fuck, I didn't like the feeling of connection with someone I'd just had sex with—it threw me off, made me anxious.

"Am I feeling like the biggest creep in the world?" Lance bit out. "Yeah, I am."

"What?" I asked, genuinely shocked.

"I took advantage of a situation." Lance ran his hands over his face. "And that may not even be the worst part." He huffed out a breath. "Look, I'm not used to this. I'm sorry I let it get to this point."

Panic coursed through my veins. "But we're good,

right?" I was willing to let this happen over and over, but only if it meant keeping Lance in my life.

"We're good." He paused. "I think." He ran a hand through his hair. "I think I just need some time. I kinda feel like shit."

Staring at him for what felt like years, I nodded. "Drink a bunch of water to wash out the toxins."

Lance cocked a brow.

"From the massage."

He nodded.

"Just so you know, I don't feel cheapened or taken advantage of. This was good, it was completely consensual, and I'm willing to let it happen again."

Lance scoffed. "Gee, thanks. Nothing like fucking your best friend's son and getting upgraded from casual, one-time dick to casual, part-time dick."

My heart clenched in my chest. I didn't like seeing Lance upset, especially not with me.

Chapter 8
Lance

It had been a week since the massage and sex.

A week since my biggest regret.

And yet, I couldn't make myself forget it. Couldn't will it from my mind.

I was pissed off.

Selfishly, it felt like I'd given in.

Like I'd lost a challenge.

Like Hudson had gotten his way, and I was left to pick up the pieces.

But, deep in my gut, I knew I'd do it again in a heartbeat.

Which was why I'd been making myself scarce around Hudson.

We'd talked a bit, but I kept it business-only when he tried to bring up the possibility of making this a casual thing. When Hudson would show up, I'd find myself suddenly busy and needing to do something elsewhere.

It was exhausting—mentally and emotionally because I *wanted* to be near him, but it felt like the only way I could keep the distance Hudson longed for.

I hated it.

"Okay, you've been avoiding me for a week," Hudson said, cornering me in the office of the Sweet & Creamy one day when I'd zipped away from him at lunch with the excuse of having paperwork to file. "Did I completely fuck things up between us?"

I closed my eyes. "Honestly, I don't know."

"Was it not good?"

"It was amazing, that's not the issue."

"What's the issue?"

Laughing bitterly, I said, "Where do we start?"

Hudson stood close, his heat and scent overwhelming me. He must have taken my question as rhetorical because he didn't answer. Instead, he stepped closer, sending every cell in my body into alert mode. "What's the worst part?"

"Huh?" My brain struggled to compute what he was asking.

"Last week," Hudson said. "You said you felt like you took advantage of me, but that wasn't even the worst part. What's the worst part?" His words were so earnest, his eyes intense.

Maybe this was my chance to break through that part of him haunted by his past. Clearing my throat, determined to be open and honest—it was the only way I wanted to start this thing with Hudson if he'd give us a chance—I said, "The worst part." Stopping, I tried to form the right words. "The worst part is...I want more. I feel like shit about what happened, but I can't stop wanting more."

Hudson's eyes lit up. "Then we're on the same page." He reached for me, pulling me close. I stopped him with a hand on his chest. "What?" he asked.

"I want more—but I want *all* of it. I want those kisses you don't share with others. I want dates and holding hands and giving things a chance to go somewhere, to build a future."

Hudson sighed, pressing his forehead to mine. "You know I can't give you that."

"Can't? Or won't?" The heat of his body, the scent that made him *Hudson* and haunted my dreams, engulfed me, tempting me to say fuck it all.

"That's not fair. You know what she did. You know how I feel about this."

"What your mom did to you—to your dad and Henry—was shit." I kept my eyes closed, breathing him in. "But one person doing a shitty thing doesn't mean everyone will do a shitty thing. I'm here for good. I want something with you. It's absolutely insane—thinking of getting involved with my best friend's son—but nothing in my life has felt more right."

"Can't we just keep things fun while we can?" Hudson's face was pinched.

"I can't," I said, stroking my fingers through his hair. "What happened between us, what I feel, it's too much for me. I can't do that again. I won't—not until it's real and forever."

Hudson's breath caught. "Nothing is forever. Everybody leaves," he whispered.

"Not everybody."

"If I don't stay, they can't leave," he whispered his little mantra, almost as if trying to remind himself. "I wasn't good enough for my mom to stick around. Why should I believe you would?"

"I guess you'd just have to trust me and find out."

For one hopeful moment, I thought Hudson was going to give in. Say he was willing to give us a chance. Instead, he just shook his head. "I'm sorry." His ragged words scraped over me. "I can't risk it."

I took a shaky breath and pulled away from him. "That's okay. I have to respect your choice. We can be friends; I'd rather be friends and work together than lose you in my life."

Hudson nodded. "Yeah, me too."

My words were the truth. I really would rather he be in my life as just a friend than not at all.

But that didn't mean I wasn't going to do every single thing in my power to win him over. Hudson had a huge loss in his life. He had a hole in his heart. I was determined to show him that not all relationships ended in pain—and I needed him by my side as we both learned what true love was.

I knew I had my work cut out for me, but I was up for the challenge.

Hudson was worth it.

And even if we didn't end up together, he still deserved to know he was good enough for love.

I wanted to be the one who gave him that gift.

It took me about one week to put together a plan and another week to set things into motion.

During that time, Hudson and I worked side-by-side.

Almost like nothing had changed.

No matter where we were, the shop, the store, the bar, the orchard, we flirted more than we had before. I don't know if it was a way to cover for what had happened between us or if it was just a natural happening between two people who were drawn to each other.

The flirting was absolute torture, but also so damn fun.

Henry noticed it for sure, but he just shot a smile and a shake of his head our way.

Casey Joe was so wrapped up in his own grief, he didn't seem to notice much of anything. I'd spent a lot of time with my friend, but I wasn't sure he was getting any better. He had a lot going for him, but until he was ready to get out of the blackness, nothing I said or did could pull him out.

Each day that passed, each day that found me working side-by-side with him, I fell harder and deeper for Hudson.

There was no question in my mind he was my person.

It didn't make sense to feel what I felt for someone so much younger than me, but there was no getting around it. What I felt for Hudson was more than anything I'd felt for anyone in my life. Not just infatuation. Not a crush. It was real and all-consuming.

And I remained committed to convincing him he could trust me—showing him that real love was worth the risk.

"You still good with me stealing Hudson away a little early tonight?" I asked Henry.

He threw a disgruntled look my way. "What?" He glanced at his hands and curled his lip. "Oh, yeah, sorry. Someone or something has been going through the trash. Made a huge mess and I've got garbage juice all over me."

I wrinkled my nose. "Gross. Animal?"

"That's what I thought at first, but animals usually eat pretty much anything they find. This seemed to be picked through." Henry washed his hands. "Never mind, sorry, what were you saying?"

"Still willing to help me get Hudson away early today?"

Henry smirked. "You remember he doesn't date, right? I don't know how you think you're going to get him to agree to a date."

"He's not going to know it's a date," I said with a shrug. "It's an undercover date."

"You're going to *trick* him into a date?"

"That's the plan."

Henry eyed me. "I don't see how it's going to work, but yeah, I'll tell him to head out early and you can do what you need to do."

Hudson walked into the main bar from the back a couple minutes later. "What's up with the trash?" he asked. "Looks like some panicked kid went through each bag searching for a retainer or something."

I chuckled, nostalgia washing over me as I recalled a very frantic Hudson searching through the trash for his retainer back when he was about thirteen. I'd had garbage up to my elbows, but we'd found it and Casey Joe had been none the wiser.

"Yeah," Henry huffed, "I don't know. Kinda worried we've got a hungry person dumpster diving, but they've been getting in the bags by the door before I even get them to the dumpster." He frowned. "Hate the idea someone is that hungry."

If I knew Henry the way I thought I did, he'd start setting out covered plates of food on the picnic table out back if he had even the slightest thought there was someone in need of food.

Hudson's eyes softened as he watched his brother, and I knew we'd had the same thought. "Well, at least it's warm right now. Would hate for you to have to give them five blankets instead of the pillow and two blankets I can already see you planning on."

Henry's cheeks pinked, but he didn't deny what we all knew he'd been thinking.

Hudson slapped his brother on the shoulder. "Lance and I were going to go over some paperwork—the swag items have sold like hotcakes, we've gotta get some more ordered and go through inventory—but I can help in about an hour if that sounds good."

Henry, seemingly lost in thought, was quiet for a moment. I cleared my throat and he jerked out of his fog. "Huh?"

"I can help in about an hour?" Hudson repeated.

"Oh, um, don't need you today. I told Darla she could have her daughter come in and help for some extra cash. The girl's going on a vacation with friends and needs to some spending money."

"I'm sure there's something I can do," Hudson said.

"Nah, take a break. You deserve it, been working your ass off."

Hudson looked annoyed, but he just nodded. "Yeah,

okay." He made his way to the back muttering something about *what the hell am I supposed to do with a break?*

A few minutes later, he reappeared with two colas in icy glasses and nodded toward our usual table in the back. "You hungry? Or just the Coke?"

I shook my head. My plan involved food, but not until later. "I'm good, thanks."

We settled into the booth and spread out our paperwork.

The numbers and conversation flowed easily, and I mostly forgot the fact I'd had my hands on his body, his mouth on my cock, and my dick buried in his ass.

Almost.

I was trying really hard, but I wasn't dead.

When we finished up—the books matched, we'd made an amazing profit, and we had a definite need to order new merchandise—I tucked everything away in my bag and moaned a yawn.

"You're damn lucky you get a break," I said. "You do deserve it."

Hudson crossed his arms over his chest and scowled. "Don't need a damn break. What am I supposed to do with a break? Take a bubble bath?"

I chuckled. "For someone who knows the importance of *others* taking time for themselves, you kinda suck at it for yourself." I *did* want Hudson to learn how to relax, but right then, I was counting on him not wanting to.

"Just feels like I'm wasting time if I'm resting or relaxing," he grumbled.

"Well, I've got a shit-ton of errands to run if you feel

like joining me," I said, hoping I sounded nonchalant. "But I'll warn you now, you'll probably be bored."

Hudson threw his notebook into his bag and beamed. "No more bored than I'd be stuck at home trying to meditate or some shit."

I laughed. "You do know that taking a break can be as simple as reading a book, watching a movie, or having a beer on the front porch, right? Doesn't have to be meditation or yoga or crocheting an afghan."

"Yeah, whatever, I'd still rather run errands. Let's go."

Score.

"We can take my truck," I offered as we exited the bar into a bright, hot Haven Grove summer.

Hudson and I climbed into my late-model Ford truck and set off.

The first stop was the hardware store to grab parts for some of the machines at the Sweet & Creamy. Hudson chatted about the peach trees and ended up buying repair parts for his irrigation system—which not only kept the orchard alive during drought conditions, but also provided frost and freeze protection—and the wind machines he'd put in near the youngest portion of the orchard. The wind machines had been a hefty investment, even more so than the irrigation system Billy had splurged on, but both were absolutely necessary to keep the trees and fruit healthy. The only thing that could wipe out a grove of peach trees faster than a hard freeze was disease or hail, and Hudson had slowly been adding netting over the most vulnerable portions of the orchard to protect from the latter.

"Didn't tell many people about the bacterial spot

because I didn't want folks to worry," Hudson said as we loaded our purchases into the truck. "But Billy'd missed it or just didn't care, so when I took over, it looked like it could have been the end of us. Got that farmer from down south to check it out and he gave me some advice. Looks like we saved it, based on how good the trees look now. Guess we'll just have to keep an eye on it. Now, if we can get through with no late-season frosts or summer hailstorms, we'll be golden."

I absolutely loved listening to Hudson talk about his work, especially the peaches. He may not have thought himself a peach farmer, but it was in his blood—whether he realized it or not—and he was damn good at it, even if it got foisted on him.

"I need to pick up some groceries, you wanna go or head back to get your truck?" I asked.

Hudson gestured toward the highway exit. "I might as well pick up some shit too. I try to buy most of my stuff from the shop if I can, but sometimes the big discount stores are just smarter for the money."

We found ourselves sharing a cart, wandering around the discount store as we talked about Henry, Casey Joe, Haven Grove, and our businesses. I couldn't help thinking about what it would be like if we were together, buying groceries for our shared place. On a real date night—one Hudson knew was happening and wanted to be on.

"I've got a cooler in the truck, we can grab some ice if we need to keep anything cold," I suggested.

"I'm good. I'll get my milk at the shop."

"You still like whole milk?" I asked, remembering the toe-headed kid who refused any milk other than whole-fat.

Hudson wrinkled his nose. "I prefer *real* milk. Let me guess, you still like that milk-water shit?"

I laughed. "Skim milk *is* real milk, it's just free of the fat."

"Free of fat, free of flavor, free of anything that makes it actual milk," Hudson said. "Remember you trying to make me eat my cereal with that when Henry and I stayed at your place one weekend? Might as well have just poured water on the Frosted Flakes."

"When you're my age, you have to sacrifice for your health," I said, only partly teasing.

Hudson scoffed. "Whatever. First, this was back when you were younger than I am now. You didn't need to sacrifice anything. Second, look at you. You're clearly healthy. It's okay to admit you just like shitty milk."

I didn't mind the compliment or the zing of desire it sent through me, and I didn't miss the heat in Hudson's eyes.

In the checkout line, I grabbed a share-size bag of chips, M&Ms, and two sodas. If Hudson noticed, he didn't say anything—probably assumed I wanted a snack at home. We split up our groceries, paid our bills, and headed out to the truck.

The day was beyond warm—not an all-out scorcher, but hot enough we were both sweating by the time we finished loading our groceries. I'd gone ahead and gotten ice for the cooler, so I threw the sodas and chocolate in, along with a few cold items I'd picked up in the store.

"Damn, it's hot," Hudson complained as I pulled the truck out of the parking lot.

"Yeah," I agreed. "Sorry, the truck doesn't have the

greatest air conditioning." I pointed toward the movie theater. "Remember the time I took you and Henry to watch X-Men that summer? You two just about froze to death and I ended up getting a blanket from my truck to cover you up while you wiped butter all over your shorts and slurped your drinks."

Hudson laughed. "I remember." He wiped at his brow. "Damn, if this is what it feels like now, hate to see it as the summer goes on. Movie theater air conditioning sounds good right about now."

I gestured with my chin toward the marquee. "They only play old stuff now, but tickets are just two dollars on weekdays. Wanna go watch," I paused and squinted, pretending to read the sign—like I hadn't already checked to see what was playing and been thrilled that fate lined it up to be Hudson's favorite movie from way back when— "um, looks like Jeepers Creepers. Didn't you like that movie when you were a kid?"

"No way," Hudson said, dipping his head to look at the movie theater marquee. "That's my favorite scary movie. Got the flower tattoo and everything."

I'd rolled my eyes back when eighteen-year-old Hudson had gotten the Jeepers Creepers flower tattoo inked around his belly button. I hadn't been rolling my eyes at the few glimpses I'd caught of the ink ever since coming back to town.

"Wanna go cool off and relive your childhood?" I asked, doing my best to play it cool.

"I was only eleven when it came out, definitely shouldn't have been watching it," Hudson said, lost in memories. "But Dad wasn't super stringent on that type of stuff, and you pretty much let Henry and me do whatever we wanted as long as Dad didn't flat-out say no. Billy wasn't paying much attention. So, Henry and I scared ourselves shitless watching it. Kept up with all the other titles that came out, too."

Taking his nostalgic jabbering as a yes, I pulled into the theater parking lot and killed the engine. I wasn't sure it would have been as easy to get Hudson to watch a movie with me if the theater hadn't been playing this one, so I threw up a quick thank you to anyone listening and grabbed the sodas from the cooler.

"Can we take these in?" Hudson asked.

"Yeah, they don't check. Here." I handed him a bottle and the candy while I took a bottle and the chips.

Heat from the blacktop seeped into our shoes as we crossed the blazing parking lot. Summer in Haven Grove was *hot*, but the temperature was above average for this time of the year. "You think this heat is gonna hurt the peaches?" I asked.

"Nah, they're a lot more at risk of disease, hail, or freeze than the heat. We've got the trunks and exposed branches whitewashed so they're good."

"Here, hold this, I'll pay. I've got a five and I'll drop a twenty in the tip jar to keep them from noticing our snacks." I handed the chips and drink to Hudson.

"Thought you said they don't check," he whispered, trying to hide the bottles and packages.

Chuckling, I pulled a five from my pocket. "I mean, they don't search bags, but I'm sure they'd have something to say if I put a soda right up there on the ticket counter."

Hudson tucked the bottles under one arm, shoved the M&Ms in his back pocket, and attempted to shield the chips in his hand. "Well, hurry up, I feel like I'm smuggling contraband."

I laughed and headed toward the outside ticket window while Hudson loitered by the door. With a smile and a thank you to the girl who popped her gum and handed over the tickets, I dropped the twenty into the tip jar. Joining Hudson by the door, I pulled it open and let my fingers just barely graze the small of his back as he walked past me.

"Oh god," he said with a moan. "It's like heaven." The cold air washed over us as we took in the tiny concession counter with bottled water, two types of canned soda, and packaged popcorn. "Damn, how does this place stay in business with two-dollar tickets?"

I shrugged. "They play old movies, I doubt it costs much to play them. They only have two screens—they play one kid movie every three days and one adult movie. Saturday has a children's matinee and a date-night movie. I drove over here my first night back home, wanted to see how things around us had changed or stayed the same. I think it's kinda a staple here because the whole theater was packed. I don't know how they'll stay open with prices everywhere going up, but they seem to be making do for now."

"Well, as long as they can keep the air on, I'm in." Hudson lifted his chin toward the Jeepers Creepers sign, and I led the way, dropping our ticket stubs in the slot where a person should have been standing. "Guess they save money by keeping a skeleton crew," Hudson said, following me into the dark theater.

As much as I *wanted* to sit in a far, back corner and make out like horny teens, the movie theater on our first not-a-date date wasn't the time or place. Hudson was all for the physical stuff, he needed to see how good we could be with the *other* side of things as well.

He glanced down toward the front, chuckled, shook his head, and pointed toward two empty seats about midway up. I nodded and followed.

"What was funny?" I asked when we settled into our seats.

Hudson scoffed. "Just remembering how much Henry and I liked to sit way down close when we were kids. Hell, if I did that now, I'd have a crick in my neck for a damn week."

"I'd have a headache within minutes," I said, shivering at the thought of sitting in the front row.

The theater filled up quickly and, as the first round of previews came on, there were only a couple seats left unoccupied.

"Maybe they do all right," Hudson said, taking in the large number of people. He nodded toward the screen. "And the advertising for local businesses between previews is a great idea."

As soon as his words were out, we both stared at each other.

"We should do that," we said at the same time and then laughed.

"Grab that number when the next ad comes on," I told him.

We devoured the bag of Cheetos before the previews were even over, our hands bumping gently as we took turns digging out handfuls. Soon, the chips were gone and we both opened our sodas and took long drinks. Hudson tore open the M&Ms and poured some in my cupped hand before settling in to pick through his. Like lightning, I recalled his habit of eating only the brown M&Ms.

"You still do that?" I asked, sifting through my handful and moving the brown ones to his hand.

He shrugged. "The brown ones seem more natural."

"You know they use dye on the brown ones too, right?"

He grinned. "Just let me enjoy my chocolate in peace."

I shook my head and took the colorful candies he offered me as the final preview came on screen.

When the actual movie started, Hudson sighed, settled back in his seat, and turned a grin my way. "This is gonna be epic."

My heart soared. Spending time with Hudson, even if he thought it was just a day of errands and staying cool in a dark theater, was everything to me. The fact he was excited to watch Jeepers Creepers—when I knew he'd seen it at least fifty times over the years—*and* he was relaxed and doing something that wasn't considered work, meant the day was an absolute success.

Getting to watch the movie I'd only seen once or twice with Hudson by my side was icing on the cake.

The first time his finger brushed mine, I thought it was likely an accident. But when he continued to make contact throughout the movie, I couldn't help but smile. Hudson may have wanted to claim he didn't do relationships, didn't want to be involved with romance, had no desire to take things further with anyone—but he was an absolute romantic at heart.

We didn't hold hands—despite how badly I wanted to wrap our fingers together—but we teased and flirted, tiny caresses of fingers, bumps of elbows, shoulders brushing. Hudson mouthed lines of the movie the whole way through and chuckled at me when I jumped at a few parts.

By the time the movie ended, I knew I'd never watch Jeepers Creepers again without my heart warming and thinking of Hudson. I'd never thought of myself as a hopeless romantic, but my heart had already traveled to the future where we celebrated each year with Cheetos, M&Ms, soda, and Jeepers Creepers while holding hands and wondering what we did before we found each other.

"You good?" Hudson asked, pulling me from my imagination. I was so fucked.

"Huh? Yeah," I answered quickly. "Just haven't watched that in years. There were parts I'd forgotten."

"I love scary movies and there are some that would definitely give that one a run for its money, but I have to say it stays at the top of my list—probably because of the memories it brings back," Hudson said as we walked out of the theater, a blast of hot air taking our breaths. "Fuck, it's hotter than when we went in."

I laughed. "Or it feels that way since we've been sitting in ice-cold air for nearly three hours." Glancing at my phone and sending up a prayer that I could get one more win for the day. "I know we had snacks, but I'm starving.

You okay if we stop at that steak place on the edge of town before we head back home?"

Hudson's stomach growled and we both laughed. "Yeah, sounds good."

I pointed the truck toward the steakhouse and we chatted about the movie and the three that followed in the franchise. Once we got to the restaurant and settled into our tiny booth at the back of the place—I said another thank you to whoever was listening for this being the only table open when we walked in because Hudson and I were pressed together at the tiny table on the rounded booth bench—Hudson cleared his throat. "You think Dad is doing worse?"

I took a long sip of water. "Yeah, I do. He didn't look good when I got back, but I think he's looking worse now."

Hudson nodded. "Henry and I were talking about it. He used to at least hit the gym, but I haven't seen him do much other than drink beer and eat pizza ever since Billy died." He scanned the menu and said thanks to the kid who brought us a basket of bread. "After you left, he went on a couple dates, but always refused to talk about them, so I figured he was either just hooking up or they turned out terrible."

I snorted. "He did that before I left too, you would have been too young to know what he was doing. But nights you and Henry got to spend with Billy or me usually meant he was on a date." I tore off a piece of bread and slathered it in butter. "I don't think he was *looking* for love, but I think he would have been happy to find a partner if it worked out that way."

Hudson was quiet for a while. "I know we can't force him to get help or make better choices, he has to be the one to decide and commit, but I'm worried about him. He's not healthy." He shook his head. "I'm the last one to talk when it comes to moving on after what our mom did, but I wish he'd at least get himself out there and a bit healthier. He deserves to be happy, but he won't ever get that if he ends up having a heart attack at fifty-three." He ran a hand over his face. "Sorry, that's morbid, but it's where my head's been lately."

I shook my head. "No, I get it. You're right. We're not getting any younger and our health doesn't come as easy as it once did. Maybe I'll see if he wants to take a run or hit the gym."

Hudson wrinkled his nose. "The gym is a hell-hole."

"True," I agreed. "Maybe we'll start with just walking through the orchard."

Our waitperson came to take our order.

"You know he doesn't go into the orchard unless it's an absolute must, right?" Hudson asked.

I nodded. "Yeah, I know he's got a thing about the orchard. But we can walk the perimeter at least."

Hudson shredded his napkin. "He used to tell us about how he fell in love with Mom in the orchard. It was a summer night with a cool breeze blowing in ahead of a storm. The moon was full and Missy sang 'It Must Have Been Love' by Roxette." Hudson gave a humorless chuckle. "Back then, I listened to that song a thousand times thinking about how much in love they must have been. I figured out when I got older that the song was a bad omen to begin with." He crumpled up the napkin scraps. "As a kid, I wanted that big, true love I thought they had. Then I realized they were doomed as early as the first night Dad fell for her—at least that story smartened me up to avoid their mistakes."

Our food arrived and we started eating. "Their mistakes aren't yours. Their fate isn't yours."

Hudson scoffed. "How could they not be? They made me, I'm part of them."

I shook my head. "They were young. Missy was messed up. She messed your dad up. What happened between them isn't your fault or your destiny."

Hudson was quiet for a while. "Well, it's not like I'm going to fall in love and dance by moonlight in the peach orchard," he joked, but his words were gruff.

I let it go and we enjoyed our meal.

"This is good," Hudson said, "but don't tell Henry. The roadhouse is great, but sometimes it's nice to get food elsewhere."

"Stepping away is good," I said. "But coming home...it just feels right."

Hudson's bright eyes met mine and he just nodded.

We split the bill—I had no idea how to get Hudson to agree to let me pay for dinner—and climbed into the truck.

"Good day?" I asked.

Hudson sighed. "Yeah, a lot better than sitting around doing nothing."

"Well, at least you got to relax a bit," I said.

"I didn't—" He cut off. "Damn, guess I did. Okay," he said with a chuckle, "it wasn't too bad."

"Tell me again why you don't date?" I asked, biting my

inner cheek to keep from smiling as my old truck carried us closer to home.

"Can't trust it," Hudson said. "Sounds good in theory, but then feelings get involved. It's best to just avoid dating at all costs."

"What's a date in your mind?"

He shrugged. "I don't know. Going somewhere together? Movie? Dinner?"

"Mmhm," I hummed.

He was quiet for a moment and then he huffed out a chuckle. "You fuckin' dirty bastard, you tricked me into a date."

"Did you have a good time?" I asked.

Hudson pursed his lips. "Fuck you, yeah, I did."

I laughed. "Mission accomplished."

When I dropped him at his truck, Hudson got out, grabbed his groceries, and walked around to my window. "Thanks, I guess. Maybe dates with you wouldn't be so bad."

I cocked a brow.

"Not committing to anything."

"Of course, not," I said with a smirk.

He knocked a fist against my truck door before heading to his truck.

"Hudson?" I said, my words like gravel.

"Yeah." He threw a look over his shoulder.

"I had fun," I said.

"Me too."

"I'd do it again in a heartbeat."

His brows drew together, but then he broke into a grin. "Yeah, well, we'll see. I don't date..."

I raised both brows.

"But for you, my gay ass might not turn down another dinner and movie," he said before biting his lip and turning toward his truck.

I floated all the way home like a damn teenager—like I wasn't over half a century old just asking to get my ass handed to me by falling for my best friend's son.

Chapter 9
Hudson

LANCE INGRAM WAS MAKING IT DAMN FUCKING hard to stick to my no dating, no relationships policy.

That damn piece of shit had tricked me into a date, and the worst part was I'd loved every second of it. It had been a week since our trick date and I hadn't been able to wipe the smile from my face.

Smiling over guys wasn't my thing. Thinking about them long after the sex wasn't something I did. I didn't normally hear certain songs and think of a guy. My usual was sex and move on. Sex and move on. Sex and move on. None of this swirly feeling in my chest—I'd never really understood the word *giddy*, but I damn sure did now.

And it was all fucking Lance's fault.

Why couldn't we just keep the sex going and enjoy it while it lasted? Why did Lance have to go and make me get all swoony over him? And it was just a damn movie and steaks—it wasn't like he took me to Paris to wine and dine me. Yet, my stupid ass was grinning like a damn fool any time I thought of our fingers brushing together or the thought he'd put into making the day happen.

So swoony.

And kinda feverish.

Or maybe I was dizzy.

"Man, you don't look so hot," Henry said as I ate lunch at the bar and went over some paperwork for the Juicy Peach while thinking about Lance.

"Just a headache," I muttered. I actually kinda felt like shit—achy, shivery, headache, exhausted.

"Your cheeks look like you've got a fever," Henry said again, reaching a hand to touch my forehead. "You're burning up. Go home and sleep."

"I'm fine."

"Damn it, Hudson, go home before you get me or my customers sick."

I glanced up with a frown, my sluggish brain not completely caught up with the conversation.

"Seriously, go home. I've got enough going on here with the trash bandit—"

"That's still a thing?" I asked.

"Yeah, but I'm just leaving food on plates now. Whoever it is has started using the blankets and pillow I left out. They're eating at the booth out back," Henry said, referring to the old booth he'd moved to the patio area outside the backdoor, "and they must be curling up there to sleep. They keep everything neat and tidy."

"Just stay out there and catch them," I muttered, not really into the conversation as a chill ran through me.

"I mean, I'm not trying to *catch* anyone. Not like they're in trouble. Wouldn't mind helping them, but I don't want to spook them and have them run away. If they're eating food and sleeping, I at least know they're somewhat safe. Haven Grove isn't dangerous. Maybe I'll meet them at some point."

"Could call the marshal," I said, my teeth chattering.

"Why? I don't want them in trouble. As long as they aren't hurting anything or doing anything illegal, I don't mind it." Henry pointed a finger at me. "Get out of here. You're sick."

"S'posed to meet with Lance," I slurred. "Gotta look at numbers."

"I'll tell him you're sick. Dad and I will take care of the orchard and the store for a few days. Go. Home. Don't come back here until the fever has broken. If it gets worse, get to the doctor."

I didn't remember packing up my bag or driving home, but I woke several hours later to a dark house, drenched in sweat, and miserable.

God, I hated being sick. Pulling myself from bed and hobbling to the bathroom, I took a piss and contemplated a shower. I was gross and sweaty, but I definitely didn't think I could stand long enough to shower. I grabbed two waters, a Gatorade, and ibuprofen before crawling back in bed.

Downing the pills with a whole bottle of water, trying to ignore my throbbing head and screaming joints, I flopped onto the pillow with a groan. I'd easily slept five hours earlier, but a wave of exhaustion rolled through me, and I knew I wasn't on the mend just yet.

My eyes drifted shut and I tumbled into fever dreams.

The next time I woke, my head at least wasn't about to

crack open, and the sun peeked through the blinds. My bladder demanded a trip to the bathroom, but I paused halfway to listen. Something else had woken me.

Coffee.

A clatter of something in the kitchen.

"Henry?" I called out.

"It's me," a familiar voice replied.

"Oh, god," I groaned under my breath. Lance couldn't fucking see me like this.

What does it matter? You're just friends and it was just a one-time thing.

"Gotta piss," I mumbled toward the kitchen before making my way to the bathroom. I still felt like shit—a quick glance in the mirror proved I still *looked* like shit—but I couldn't soak in my own sweat any longer. Knowing a shower would feel great, even if it took every ounce of energy I had, I poked my head out the door. "Gonna shower real quick." I wasn't sure why Lance was in my house, but it seemed rude to leave him by himself without an explanation.

"Take your time," he said. "Holler if you need anything, don't push it. I'll have food ready if you feel like eating."

The shower had the combined effect of making me feel somewhat better—or at least less stinky—and also exhausting me to the point of my knees buckling. Wrapping the towel around my waist, and praying I could find a blanket to wrap up in so I didn't have to cuddle into slick, sweaty sheets, I made my way back to my bedroom.

And found Lance.

Lance in my bedroom.

Lance making my bed—or *remaking* my bed—with new sheets, the old ones piled in a heap on the floor. "Figured you didn't want to get back into sweaty sheets. These were in your closet, hope they're okay to use."

Unable to stand any longer, a shivery chill letting me know the fever may have gone down but it wasn't completely gone, I lost the towel and climbed under the covers. Teeth chattering, I mumbled a thank you and prayed to warm up quickly.

Sometime later, I woke with a start, pressed against Lance's thigh. What the fuck? My noodly arms protested as I tried to push into a sitting position.

Why was Lance in my bed?

"Hey," he crooned. "You've been out for a while."

"Why are you here?" I croaked.

"Wanted to make sure you were okay. Whatever bug you've got hit you quick and knocked you on your ass. I made chicken soup when you feel up to some—like the real kind to help with being sick." Lance stood from the bed. "There was no chair in here, didn't know how you'd feel about me pulling one in, so I just popped a squat." He gestured toward the kitchen. "Water? Juice? Gatorade?"

My stomach grumbled, the scent of chicken soup calling to me. "I'll get it."

"Stay in bed. You may be *better*, but you're not back to one hundred percent yet. I'll get it. Soup?"

I nodded. "Can I least go piss?"

Lance smirked as he left the room.

Somehow, after a trip to the bathroom and a bowl of chicken soup, we ended up spending the entire day together. Lance insisted I stay in bed and rest, bringing me liquids and pain pills throughout the day. At one point, I heard him washing dishes, and I swore he cleaned the bathroom and started a load of laundry.

By the time dinner rolled around, I truly did feel nearly normal—the bug had been short-lived but had knocked me out for almost forty-eight hours.

"No need to push it," Lance said. "You wanna try a shower and dinner?"

"Shower sounds great."

Thirty minutes later, I was starting to think I may be back among the living as I shuffled into the kitchen. My eyes immediately snagged on a vase of flowers. "Where'd those come from?"

Lance shrugged, plating salmon and veggies at the stove. "Thought they'd brighten things up. Everyone deserves get-well-soon flowers."

"You got me flowers?" Even I heard the awe in my voice.

Lance just gestured toward the table and brought our plates over.

We ate dinner and fell into easy conversation as if we'd been eating meals together in my farmhouse kitchen for decades. In a way, based on our history, that wasn't far from the truth. The contented easiness had built between us since the day I was born.

But the awareness, the tension sizzling between us, the pull to take what had existed for years and make it into something so much more lit a fire in my belly—urging me to make a move, admit defeat, give the spark a chance to flame to life.

Never in my life had I been so comfortable and

completely myself with someone other than family. Never had I wanted so badly to keep things exactly how they were while also *dying* to see where things could go.

We ended up in the living room with the television on low as we talked about a few business-related things. When my eyes drifted closed, I gave in to the pull of sleep for a few moments. Lance's chuckle pulled me from my slumber with a start.

"Sorry," he said with a wince, a book in hand. "Funny part." He held up the book he was reading.

"Haven't read that one yet, you like it?" I murmured. The book was a fictionalized autobiography of a top film star. It had gotten a lot of flak, but also some great reviews for the candid retelling of some of the less flattering parts of his life.

Lance flipped back a few pages and began to read.

Out loud.

Like it was fucking story time.

This gorgeous man had barged back into my life, set me on fire, thrown me for a loop, and demanded things I was sure I couldn't give.

And now, he was taking care of me while I was sick.

Cooking dinner for me.

Buying me flowers.

Helping me when I was down for the count.

And reading me a fucking book.

No one had ever read me a book. Sure, teachers at school, but no one at home. Even before Mom left, she wasn't that type of mom. Dad was too busy trying to make a miserable marriage work before she left, and too swallowed up in grief to read to me or Henry after she left.

And Henry didn't love to read so I'm sure it didn't even cross his mind to read his little brother a story.

But Lance sat right there on my couch and read me a fucking book.

The lump in my throat had to be from the virus. I needed to hydrate and get some more sleep. I cleared my throat and stood up. "Um, think I'm going to head to bed. Thanks for all you did for me. Means a lot and was a real help."

Not giving Lance time to respond, I shot toward my room and shut the door.

Staring at the ceiling, I listened to the soft sounds of Lance puttering around the house.

My house.

Lance.

The man was in my house, taking care of me as if it were the most natural thing in the world.

Despite being exhausted, sleep didn't come for a long time that night.

My brain was way too busy arguing with itself about the pros and cons of giving things with Lance a chance.

By the time morning rolled around, I knew a couple things.

One, I was well on my way to loving Lance. I mean, I'd loved him my whole life, but this was different. This was falling for the guy.

Falling.

In love?

Fuck, *in love*.

Something Hudson Riggs *did not* do.

Two, I still wasn't convinced I had it in me to give Lance what he wanted.

But my heart had finally won the battle and talked me into taking the risk.

I wasn't sure *how* to be in a relationship, but I knew for certain I didn't want to lose the chance to take that journey with Lance.

Three, I was scared as fuck.

Chapter 10

Lance

TAKING CARE OF HUDSON HAD GIVEN ME A purpose and proved to me I wanted something real with him.

Through thick and thin.

Sickness and health.

Slow down, Ingram. You're getting way too far ahead of yourself. The guy was sick and you took care of him. It wasn't a marriage proposal.

But something had changed between Hudson and me when he'd been down for the count.

Ever since the day I walked into Glazed Buns and saw him sitting there, something had sparked to life. Yeah, the sex had been amazing, but it hadn't been a true connection at that point in time.

The real intimacy had come from the hours we spent together—laughing, reliving the past, building a foundation for the future...even if Hudson was *sure* he couldn't offer me that.

Those quiet moments watching him sleep.

Making him dinner.

Buying him flowers.

Reading him a book.

Hudson thrived on being taken care of—something Casey Joe had done to the best of his ability, but not in the way a kid really needed. If Hudson would only let me in, give things between us a chance, I knew I could happily spend the rest of my life taking care of him.

Whistling while I did an early-morning clean and prep of the Sweet & Creamy for opening, I couldn't help the smile plastered across my face. I knew I had to be patient and take things slow—Hudson had to be the one to decide if this thing flaming to life between us was worth the giant leap he'd have to take.

But that didn't mean I couldn't enjoy the little moments and dream while I waited.

A bit later, as I finalized the sale paperwork—I planned on buying the shop outright from Mom once I got her to agree—the door to my office burst open, bouncing against the wall as Hudson bulldozed into the room. "What the hell is this?" he demanded, holding a piece of paper clutched in his fist.

I stood up and rounded my desk, closing the door behind him—it was still quite a while until we opened, but I didn't need anyone walking in and overhearing us. "Not sure," I answered calmly, knowing exactly what he had in his hand. "Maybe if you took yourself down a couple notches and stopped waving it around like a battle axe, I could get a better look."

"A better look?" Hudson growled. "Don't act like you

don't know what it is. You know exactly what it is. You damn dirty shit." His words had decreased in both volume and anger, the quirk of a smile playing on his lips.

Scowling, I stepped closer. "Seriously, can't see it. At my age, the eyes are the first to go," I said, fighting a smile. "Move it closer, let me get my readers."

Hudson moved into my space, an arm going around my waist, his lips only inches from mine. "You put a damn note in my lunchbox. Like I'm a fucking kid." His eyes flashed, indecision and desire at war. "And I don't know what's worse. The fact I ate that shit right up—although, I'm not sure lunchbox notes are supposed to be so sexy. Or how badly I want to throw this at your damn head and storm out of here, keep my distance, stick to the plan."

His breath tickled over my face, our hips pressed together, chests brushing with each inhale. "Go ahead," I whispered. "Throw it and storm out."

A challenge.

Hudson's eyes caught fire.

"Or," I went on, my words rough, the tension between us thick. I swallowed. "Or, just give in. Let it happen. Admit that this might not be the nightmare you're afraid it will be."

"I may be terrible at it," Hudson whispered, words catching in his throat.

"Same."

"Might need to go slow."

"I'm patient." I nuzzled my nose against his.

"Don't want to lose what we've found together," Hudson said, his words raw and real.

"What we had back then, what we have now, it's

rooted too deep to just lose it. We build on it, make it bigger and better, but the foundation—love and friendship —it stays the same." Did my voice sound as desperate as I felt—like I'd do and say anything to get Hudson to just take that step with me?

Hudson took a deep breath. "Dad..." He trailed off.

"We'll let Casey Joe in on it slowly, ease him into it." I brushed a kiss to Hudson's temple. "He loves us. Give him some time and I think he'll eventually come around."

"Really?"

"Hopefully." Pressing kisses along Hudson's jawline, I teased fingers through the hair at the nape of his neck. "What did your lunchbox note say?"

Hudson huffed a laugh. "You know damn well what it said."

"Something, something...can't stop thinking about you...something, something...want those secret kisses you don't give to others...blah, something, blah...not giving up, willing to wait, you're so much more than just sex..." I'd known the note was a leap, but it was fun and had potential, and it had paid off. "Something like that?"

"Fuck you," Hudson growled. "You waltzed in here and broke all my rules. You should be disqualified and benched."

"But?"

He buried his head in my neck with a half sob, half laugh. "But I can't get you out of my head, can't stop wanting to touch you, wanting to spend every fucking minute with you."

"What about those kisses?" I asked, teasing, but dying to taste him.

Hudson groaned, lifting his head, his pretty pink lips begging for attention. "They're yours," he whispered.

His tongue darted out to chase my thumb as I trailed it over his bottom lip. With both hands cupping his face, our lips only inches apart, I savored the moment of delicious tension before pressing our mouths together.

Sweat heat.

A gasp, a groan.

Slick, nipping, teasing.

And then the kiss morphed from sexy and playful to hot, demanding, drunk with desire-filled promises.

A kiss had never tasted so good.

Had never lit me on fire, so hot and needy.

Hudson's tongue, slick against mine, pulled a moan from deep in my chest.

Whirling him around and pressing him against my desk, I stepped between his spread legs, growling when the twin bulges behind our jeans came together.

The sweaty, salty flavor of his skin danced on my tongue as I trailed kisses along his jawline and down his neck.

Hudson whimpered when I bit lightly at the sensitive skin where his neck and shoulder met, dipping his head and bringing our mouths back together. Like a starving man, hungry for only *my* kisses, Hudson feasted on my mouth.

"Can't." He pressed a kiss to my lips. "Stop." Another kiss to my cheek. "Kissing." A brush of lips over my eyelid. "You." Back to my mouth, bruising as he crushed our lips together.

"Don't stop," I said, wishing like hell we were near a

bed. Our first time—the first time that really meant something—wouldn't be on a desk in my office.

We kissed forever.

And then we kissed some more.

Finally, Hudson broke away, panting. Pressing his forehead to mine, he took a shuddering breath. "Really want you to fuck me," he said. "But it feels like this needs to be one of those let's take it slow type things."

"If we had a bed, I'd argue with you," I said, brushing my lips over his mouth.

"No bed, no full-on sex," Hudson said, regret lacing his words. "But we can get each other off." He stood, adjusting himself, and pushed me toward the desk chair. Once I'd sat down, he went to work on my jeans, the button and zipper open in a flash. Hudson gripped the waistband of my boxer briefs and looked at me, a silent question hanging between us.

At my nod, he lifted the material, licking his lips as he uncovered my hard cock. "Fuckin' hot," he murmured, his eyes catching mine.

"Bet you say that to all the guys," I teased, meaning it to be light, but the streak of white-hot jealousy shooting through me was anything but.

"Haven't been with anyone since you," Hudson said. "You fucked me up for anyone else."

"I didn't—" My words cut off with a hiss when Hudson wrapped his lips around my cockhead and swirled his tongue. "Fuck, Hudson."

He worked me over for several minutes, sucking and licking, his head bobbing, fist working with just the right amount of pressure. Right when I thought he'd finish me off, Hudson stood, wiping pre-cum and spit from his chin. "My turn."

He started to undo his pants, but I pushed him to lean against the desk and batted away his hands. I lifted the edge of his t-shirt until Hudson got the clue and took it off enough to catch behind his neck. Rolling the desk chair closer, my dick and balls throbbing, I pressed kisses against the flower tattoo adorning his belly button. Making quick work of his button and zipper, I found Hudson's hot pink boxer briefs soaked through and his dick bulging against the fabric. Mouthing along the outline of his cock, I savored the warm, musky scent and the steely heat under my lips.

"Suck me," Hudson demanded, his words flaming the fire in my blood.

Shifting his underwear to catch below his balls, I gripped his cock and flicked my tongue over his slit. I wasn't a complete novice when it came to giving head, and I definitely knew what felt good, but Hudson's eyes on me as I took his cock deep to the back of my throat was a new thrill I hadn't even known I needed.

I liked him watching me, liked knowing it was my mouth, my tongue, my hand urging those grunts and groans from him. Liked the way his fingers slipped into my hair and tugged me gently, his hips rocking, the head of his dick going deeper and deeper in my throat.

When I gagged, Hudson cursed and pulled out of my mouth. "I'm sorry," he said, pulling me up to stand. "Fuck, your mouth is so good," he whispered, his lips against mine, the flavor of our pre-cum and cocks mixing together. "Pull your pants down," he demanded.

Loving the way Hudson took charge, I shucked my pants and underwear down, chuckling when he pushed me to sit in the desk chair. He stripped out of his pants and underwear in one smooth motion, leaving the t-shirt caught behind his neck, emphasizing gorgeous pecs and dusky-pink nipples I wanted to get my mouth on. Toeing the wheel lock on the chair, Hudson studied the arms. "Do these collapse?"

Blinking away the haze of lust, I glanced at the arms of the chair. "Um, yeah, I think so." I pressed a button at the back of one arm and it lurched forward to position itself out of the way. When I'd done the same with the other arm, Hudson smiled and straddled me, wrapping his arms around my neck as our cocks rubbed together.

"Can you come like this?" he asked.

I grunted and pulled him in for a long, sloppy, hot kiss, one hand trailing down his back to grip his ass. Hudson rocked his hips, riding me, pressing his cock against mine, our pre-cum leaking against our bellies. "Fuck, yeah," I said.

"Help me," Hudson begged, his hand wrapping around our dicks and stroking. "Jack us off."

With our hands stroking together, both of us teasing thumbs over our leaking slits, we set a rhythm I knew I wouldn't be able to keep up with for long. Leaning in, I took one of Hudson's nipples in my mouth and sucked, swirling my tongue around the tight bud.

He cursed and thrust into my fist, the hot friction between our dicks building higher and higher to our release.

"Want you in my hole," Hudson whispered, his lips

against my ear as we let loose of the double stroking and jerked our own dicks in a desperate frenzy. "Wanna feel you come in me."

"Next time," I said, stroking my throbbing cock as I imagined sliding into Hudson's ass and making him mine. "Real bed, real feelings." My words were babble, but I didn't care.

"Yes," Hudson agreed on a whimper. "Fuck, yes. Oh god, Lance, I'm so close. Gonna come."

"Come on me," I demanded, my own balls drawn up tight, ready to explode.

With a groan, Hudson came all over my chest and stomach, his balls pressed against me. The hot splash of his load on my skin was enough to send me over the edge. My release shot hot and thick between us, our cum mixing together as he leaned in to capture my mouth.

We kissed for several long, slow moments until we'd caught our breaths.

"Um, we're a mess," Hudson said with a lazy smile against my mouth.

I leaned forward and pulled open a desk drawer to grab a box of tissues.

With a quick cleanup—or the best we could do with tissues—we silently dressed again. Was this when Hudson would freak out? Was he just waiting for the right moment to bolt?

"Is it weird how much I liked being taken care of when I was sick?" Hudson asked, his words barely a whisper. "Like, how fucked am I that a friend doing nice things for me got me all up in my feels?"

I pulled him into a hug. "We all like being taken care

of. You just missed out on it a bit more than some, so it means even more. There's nothing bad or weird about it."

"Would have bet money I didn't need shit like that," he said.

"Sometimes we don't know what we need until it's right in front of us." I ran my hand up and down his back. "What you said earlier, about not being with anyone else." I drew back and made sure Hudson's eyes met mine. "I'd never make you stop the massage stuff—I can't say I'd *like* knowing you were doing that with other guys, but I wouldn't presume—"

"Shut up," Hudson said, his face breaking out into a huge grin. "You're ridiculous. Why do you think I haven't had any hookups or massages lately?"

I shrugged, something akin to surly teen taking over.

"I went and met some hot-ass guy in a coffee shop and got my head and dick all wrapped up in him."

My eyes came up to meet his. "Just your head and dick?"

Hudson leaned in to kiss me. "Maybe my heart too. Look, I may not have any experience with this real shit, but I know enough to know that I don't want you sleeping around and I don't have any need to sleep around if we're going to do this. So, the hookups are done while this is happening. The regular massages are still a thing, but I won't be taking any *full-service* appointments if we're together."

"Why do you keep saying *if*?"

"I mean, we *are*. Right? This is where things get weird for me. I don't know how to do this. This is why I've always avoided getting involved."

"Let's just say we're together and we're taking things slow, seeing where things go." I cupped his face and brushed a soft kiss over his lips. "How's that?"

"I can work with that," Hudson said, gripping the back of my head and deepening the kiss. "But now, I need to go home and shower before I go help Henry at the bar. You coming in for dinner?"

"It's a date," I said, smacking his ass as he walked toward the door. "Hudson?"

"Yeah," he said, eyes bright as he turned to face me.

"I know we're going slow—whatever that means for you is fine by me—but if you wanted to, I don't know, have a sleepover sometime soon, I wouldn't say no."

He grinned and bit his lip. "That's good information to know."

Once Hudson was gone, I headed upstairs and cleaned up. Unable to wipe the smile from my face, I flopped onto my bed and relived the moments with Hudson. When my eyes fluttered shut, I grabbed my phone, set an alarm for thirty minutes, and let sleep take over.

"Where's Hudson?" Henry asked with a frown.

"Whatdya mean?" I asked as I sat at the bar. "Thought he was here. Said he had to help you tonight." The lights flickered as lightning flashed outside and the bar shook from the roll of thunder. "Damn, that's building up to be one heck of a storm."

"Seriously, he's not with you?" Henry demanded.

"He was," I answered, my cheeks heating. "But he left

to get ready and come here. We were going to meet for dinner."

Henry grabbed his phone and tapped a few times. "Fuck," he growled. "Damn big hail expected. He's probably out in the orchard."

"Out in the orchard? With that storm rolling in?" I pushed away from the bar, terror filling my chest. I punched my phone screen and listened to the incessant ringing until Hudson's voicemail kicked on. "Fuck. You try."

While Henry tried to call his brother, I sent a text telling him to answer his fucking phone.

Neither of us got any kind of response.

Honestly, it wasn't surprising. If he was in the orchard on a *good* day, the reception could be spotty. In the middle of a storm, reception was likely zero.

Henry glanced around at the full roadhouse.

"I'll go," I said. "Keep your phone on. I'll let you know when I find him."

"He'll be in the section that doesn't have netting, probably trying to get as many picked as possible to save them from the hail," Henry said, worry etching lines across his face. "God damn it," he growled, clearly fearing for his brother's safety.

We both winced when the windows flashed to life from lightning. The thunder roared, rattling the glasses behind the bar.

"Take my raincoat and flashlight," Henry ordered. "And when you find him, punch him in his damn stupid face for me."

I nodded, grabbed the coat from the hook on the wall,

and took the large flashlight Henry handed me. Throwing the raincoat on, grateful for the hood with the visor, I zipped it up and tied the hood tight.

"Boots," Henry said, pointing to his big, waterproof boots in the corner. "Forget your shoes, they'll be soaked in less than thirty seconds."

Toeing off my loafers, I stuck my feet in Henry's boots, glad we were nearly the same size. Pulling my phone from my pocket, I quickly shared my location with Henry and with Hudson before tucking it back into the inner pocket of the raincoat where it would hopefully stay dry.

"Be careful. That lightning is wicked. No one should be out in it," he said, worry lacing his words. "Don't be under trees, but don't be the tallest thing out there, either."

I nodded and slapped him on the back. "I'll find him." I hoped that was true. In all honesty, I was scared to death. I didn't hate storms, but I had a strong respect for them—knew the deadly damage they could bring. The good news was there were no tornadoes in this storm system. The bad news was the possible hail—but that wasn't a sure thing. The current worst part was the wind and lightning, plus the deluge of rain.

Walking into the onslaught, I took a moment to get my bearings. The rain was heavy, but it wasn't as icy cold as I'd expected. The wind nearly knocked me to my knees, but I turned toward the section of the orchard where the peaches were the most unprotected and the closest to being ready to pick.

The good thing about peaches was they could be picked a bit early and still ripen over time. No doubt in my mind that Hudson would do everything he could to get the netting rigged up over *all* of the orchard as soon as possible.

If the damned fool lived through this storm.

Every bellow of Hudson's name was drowned out by the wind and the rain, but I kept yelling, kept making my way toward where I thought he'd be. I'd known the orchard way back when, but Hudson and I had spent many recent days walking the land and talking about his plans to make the orchard and the Juicy Peach bigger and better, so I knew exactly the section he was most likely to start picking peaches.

When I reached the little lean-to, strategically placed to best withstand storm winds, a chuckle of relief escaped my chest. Inside the lean-to were about ten bushels of peaches protected from the storm. Hudson was saving his crop while risking his life.

"Fucking hell, Hudson," I growled. "No. We're not doing this. I refuse to have you finally give the go-ahead for us to take a chance and then have you break your neck or be struck by lightning for some fuzzy fruit." I laughed, a bit of hysteria seeming to eat at the edges of my mind, and swung the flashlight around.

If the baskets were here, Hudson was obviously bringing them in one at a time. I could wait until he brought the next one.

Or I could wait and wait and he'd never show because he fell off the ladder or got electrocuted.

There was no way I could just stand in that little lean-to and hope he came back with another bushel of peaches. Stepping out into the downpour, the howling winds whipping rain into my eyes, I glanced to the left and the right.

The flashlight went dim.

Flickered.

And went out.

Fuck.

Closing my eyes, I tried to feel Hudson's presence. Which way should I go?

With nothing but a gut feeling, I darted off to the right.

The ink-black night and roaring wind absorbing my desperate, repeated cries of *"Hudson!"* as I ran through the orchard.

As I rounded a row of peach trees, a body silhouetted in a flash of lightning.

"Hudson!" My screams useless in the roar of thunder.

Another flash.

The storm was right on top of us.

Flash.

Hudson's outline walking toward me.

My soul trembling as the ground shook with thunder.

And then the world went white, the atmosphere cracking, an inferno of heat as a bolt of lightning struck the orchard.

Hudson went down.

Chapter 11
Hudson

"FUCK," I MUTTERED TO MYSELF, UNABLE TO hear the curse over the howling wind and crashing thunder. The latest lightning strike had been way too close, the electric heat slapping my face, my vision whiting out.

I'd rushed into the orchard the moment my weather tracker indicated the probability of hail. Grateful I'd had the money and foresight to install the netting over the most vulnerable portions of the orchard, I was dead-set to save as much of the more unprotected crop as possible.

So far, I'd managed to fill about ten bushel baskets with peaches from the tops of the trees most likely to be ready to harvest within the next week or so. My hope was that the lower-hanging fruit would be more protected from the hail if the storm produced any.

In my heart, I knew I wouldn't be able to save the whole crop, but I couldn't just let the storm roll in without doing *something*.

Just one more. The mantra reverberated through my head like the thunder rumbling through the orchard.

One more basket.

One more.

Just.

One.

More.

In the end, I got fifteen baskets of the most vulnerable peaches into the lean-to. It wasn't all of them. Any big hail would still destroy a lot of the crop.

But I'd done something.

At least I'd done something.

Rounding a row of peach trees, I jerked in the darkness as a bolt of lightning cracked, lighting up the sky. Was there someone in the orchard? Now my damn head was playing tricks on me.

I needed to get to the lean-to.

The farmer's shed would be better. At least there, I'd have a roof and four walls. If tornadoes had been predicted, I would have worked my way toward the storm cellar, but the shed would be more comfortable in the absence of twisters. I'd spruced the place up last time I was there—adding a full-sized bed, bottles of water, and some canned peaches. Not only would it be a decent place for a nap during harvest, it was a nice little shelter in case of emergencies.

And let's be honest, if the right hookup had come along before Lance, I wouldn't have minded a bit of orchard shed fun. The place wasn't huge—very tiny-house-esque—but the closet had clean sheets and towels, the water pump was functional.

Lance.

His name flashed through my mind and my heart gave a weird flutter that had nothing to do with the proximity of lightning or the potential damage to my peaches.

Another flash of lightning and I was sure someone else was in the orchard.

Creeped out, exhausted, and realizing just how stupid I'd been to come out in a lightning storm, I increased my speed.

The farmer's shed.

It wasn't far.

Just had to get there.

I could dry off and sleep, check the damage in the morning, and get the baskets transported to the Juicy Peach to set my unplanned harvest out for ripening.

The hairs all over my body stood on end.

That was the only warning I got before my world went white-hot and I was flung to the ground. Pain jarred me as I hit the wet earth, something slamming hard against my chin. The heat so intense, the light so bright, true fear shot through me. I took a moment to get my bearings on the wet ground of the pitch-black orchard.

Rolling to my back, I groaned to see a peach tree split in two, fire attempting to burn through the rain, and smoke wafting from the blackened, sizzling mess.

"Hudson!" Lance dropped to his knees, his hands hovering over me. "Are you okay? Are you hurt? Did it hit you?"

"I knew I kept seeing someone out here, ya damn creeper," I yelled.

His relief was palpable as he leaned down and hugged

me to him. "I'm going to ream your ass for this stunt, but we need to get out of the storm," he said in my ear.

"Sounds promising," I yelled back.

I swore I heard him laughing as he helped me up. "You okay?"

"Yeah. Farmer's shed," I said, pointing uselessly in the blackness toward the little building beyond the edge of the orchard—I didn't want more lightning, but at least then we could see *something*.

I'd hit my chin *hard*, rattled my damn teeth, but luckily, I hadn't chomped down on my tongue or lips. The way my chin stung, it *had* to be gashed open, but there was nothing I could do about it right then.

We hauled ass through the storm.

Just as we reached the shed, tiny pellets of ice attacked.

"No!" I screamed, trying to pull away and go rescue more fruit.

Lance grabbed me and tackled me into the shed. We fell in a wet heap on the floor, the slight scent of mildew tickling my nose from the all-weather mat I'd placed by the door.

Struggling to get up, I clamored to get back outside.

"Damn it, Hudson, stop," Lance demanded. He pushed at my chest and threw himself against the door, blocking my way out. "Fuck, just stop. You can't go back out there."

Exhaustion and worry laced his words as the pellets of ice echoed on the shed's roof. "I didn't get them all," I mumbled, shifting to lean against him. "I could have gotten more."

Soaked to the bone, we sat huddled together as the

storm raged outside. "I know, babe, but you also could have gotten killed." Lance wrapped his arm around my neck and pulled me close. "Fuck." He let out a long, harsh breath. "I saw you in that flash of lightning and then you dropped, I thought you'd been hit." He shuddered and held me tighter. "Fuck. I thought you'd been hit."

"I'm good. It knocked me down and I hit my chin. Way too close for comfort, swear it singed me, but I'm okay."

We sat quietly as the storm continued to pound down.

"How'd you know where I was?" I asked, my teeth beginning to chatter as my rain-soaked clothes grew colder with each passing moment.

"You mean how'd I know my dumbass boyfriend had lost his damn mind and gone out to a fucking orchard in the middle of a lightning storm?" Lance demanded, fear still tingeing his words, but a bit of his usual sarcastic humor resurfacing.

"They said it could hail..." I muttered.

"I got to the bar—where we were meeting for a dinner date might I remind you—and Henry asked where you were. When we figured out you weren't where we expected you to be, and a storm was rolling in, he checked the weather. Soon as he saw hail predicted, he said you'd probably gone out to save as many peaches as you could." Lance moved and I imagined him running his hand over his face. "Swear to god, if you think you're doing this every time they predict hail, I'm going to ban you from weather forecasts."

"Once I get netting over the other sections—"

"No." He shifted, gripping the back of my head and

pulling me to his chest. "No. You're not going out in a lightning storm ever again. Do you hear me? You put yourself in danger, you put me in danger—"

"Hang on," I said, pulling away from him as my anger sparked. "I didn't make you come after me."

"No," Lance said with a sigh. "You just made me fall ass over ankles for you. Made me more concerned for you than anyone I've ever worried about in my entire life." His hand landed on my arm. "No, I didn't *have* to come after you. No, I didn't think you *couldn't* take care of yourself. But my heart was in that orchard, and I didn't know what else to do."

I took a deep breath. "Oh." I wasn't sure how to feel about what he'd said. Part of me wanted to run away in terror. But the other part of me, the part beating wildly in my heart—deep in my soul, the part fighting to claim this man as my own—that part just wanted to snuggle close to him and let him hold me.

"Yeah, *oh*," Lance said gently. "I think it's stopped," he said a few moments later.

"They said it could be severe, deadly hail," I muttered.

"And you still went out in it."

"Those peaches are our livelihood," I argued.

He sighed. "I know. Luckily it stayed small and didn't last long."

I drew in a ragged breath. "I'm sorry. I shouldn't have taken that risk for something that didn't even happen."

"Shhhh," Lance soothed into the darkness. "We should get back."

I caught his arm. "Can we just stay here a while?"

"We're soaked and you're starting to chatter," Lance said.

"Please? We have towels and there are clean sheets."

"Let me tell Henry we're okay," Lance said. He fished around in his raincoat and the room filled with light from his phone's flashlight. "Shit, he's been texting. I shared my location with you both, but it may not be picking up well." Lance tapped the screen and waited a moment. "Okay, he's glad we're safe. Says he'll punch your stupid face tomorrow."

I chuckled. "In hindsight, I realize I shouldn't have run off like that."

"Shhh, it's over. We can't change it. You're safe."

The calming silence echoed around us after the raging cacophony of the storm

"Boyfriend, huh?" The weird little thrill that word gave me was foreign as hell.

Awkward.

Scary.

And kinda exciting.

Lance chuckled. "If you're okay with it."

"It's a first, for sure."

"I like us having firsts together," Lance said, his breath soft against my ear.

I leaned in closer but hissed when my chin scraped over the seam of his jacket.

Pulling back quickly, Lance took my chin in hand and winced. "That looks sore."

"Stitches?"

"No, I think it's more a scrape and bruise than a cut."

He glanced around the little shed. "Do you have a first-aid kit out here?"

"Yeah," I said, moving to stand and pulling him up from the floor. "There should be battery-operated lanterns. There's a little hot plate we can use to warm water from the pump—as long as the generator is working. We can wash off, hang our clothes around to dry, and sleep."

We moved around the tiny shed, turning on the lanterns and hanging up our wet jackets. The boots we'd both had on would take days to dry and likely smell like wet dog and musty feet for the rest of time.

"Sit at the table," Lance said. "I'll get some water. We can start it warming up while I clean your chin."

While he went out to the pump, I grabbed the big pot and the hot plate. We wouldn't be boiling the water, but it would at least get warm for a quick wash-up. I pulled out two washcloths, two large towels, and the first-aid kit.

Before Lance returned, I turned on the generator and plugged in the hot plate. Shucking out of my wet shirt and pants, I laid them on the back of two chairs in hopes they'd be dry—or at least less soaked—by morning.

With a shiver, I rummaged in the tiny closet until I found the sheets. The full-sized bed took up the majority of the little shed, and I maneuvered around the edges as I pulled the fitted sheet over the mattress and spread the top sheet over it. The night was cooler now that the storm had rolled through, but I wasn't sure it was cool enough to warrant me digging deeper to find a quilt. I figured Lance and I could keep each other warm enough.

"Damn, that's a sight I wouldn't mind seeing every

time I walk through the door," Lance said, a grin dancing on his words as he took in the wet underwear plastered to my ass while I bent to finish the bed.

Smiling, loving the light, fluffy feeling in my chest, I moved back to the chair as Lance poured his bucket of water into the pot and sat it on the hot plate.

"Are we playing naked doctor?" Lance asked, his hot eyes traveling up and down my chest and legs.

I shrugged. "I don't know what you're doing. I'm just being pragmatic and letting my clothes dry."

"Let me clean your chin," he said. "After that, anything is fair game." He stripped out of his clothes, never taking his eyes from mine.

He hung his shirt and pants to dry.

Adjusted the waistband of his soaking wet boxer briefs.

And winked.

That fuckin' wink.

It did stupid things to my belly, and I cursed the damn blush heating my cheeks.

"Sit down," Lance ordered as he rummaged through the first-aid kit.

Legs trembling, whether because of the storm and exertion or because my boyfriend was sexy as fuck when he got bossy, I sank into a kitchen chair.

Lance tossed supplies on the table and stepped between my legs. Gripping my chin, he studied the gash in the dim light of the tiny shed. "Needs cleaned or it'll get infected. This might—"

I gasped when the peroxide-soaked gauze wiped over

the wound. "Fuck! You didn't even count down!" Hissing as he swiped over the cut again, I tried to back away.

"Sit still. There's dirt in it." He got a new piece of gauze and splashed peroxide on it. "One more, then I'll be done." It didn't sting any less the next time, but my nose caught a whiff of Lance, and all I wanted to do was press my face to his torso and breathe him in deeply.

"Maybe you should kiss it better," I said, my eyes zoned in on the thick erection now tenting his underwear.

Lance smirked and leaned in to blow softly over my chin. "Better?"

I shook my head and tapped my lips. "It hurts right here."

He lost the battle to hold back his grin and fire glowed in his grayish-green eyes. Tipping my chin, Lance brushed his lips over mine. "I think maybe you should get in bed. You don't want to catch a chill."

"A chill," I echoed, nodding solemnly. "Definitely don't want to catch a chill. I bet it would help me stay chill-free if I could find a sexy silver fox to cuddle up next to me."

Lance gently covered my injury with two small bandages before pressing a kiss to my lips. "Don't know about the sexy part, but I can provide the silver."

Snorting, I stood and shucked off my wet underwear. "You're doing just fine in the sexy department." Gesturing toward the hot plate, I said, "The water should be warm."

Lance stripped out of his underwear and tossed me one of the washcloths. "Come 'ere," he growled. Dipping the cloth into the pot of water, he squeezed out the excess and wiped the warm water over my chest and down my arms.

Wetting my cloth, I mirrored his movements.

By the time he spun me and gently washed my back, pressing kisses between my shoulder blades, I'd lost all focus on cleaning up. Every single thought was gathered in my cock.

In the dim light of the shed, we finished our own clean-up, paying attention to the more intimate areas before turning off the hot plate and spreading the washcloths out to dry.

A cool breeze blew through the window screens, and I shivered.

"See? A chill." Lance pulled down the top sheet. "Climb in."

Naked and spent from the storm, I let Lance pull my little spoon into his big spoon under the light sheet.

Sleep wasn't in my plan when I crawled into the small bed, but exhaustion combined with Lance's warm body pressed against me, and sleep won out.

When I woke sometime later, the very first streaks of pink and orange painted the sky. The shed smelled of cold and rain, but I was warm with Lance wrapped protectively around me.

Not gonna lie, the bed was cramped. We were both pretty big dudes, but having him pressed against me, holding me, was the best feeling in the world.

How had I ever thought I didn't need this?

Didn't need *him*?

Reaching behind me, I caressed a hand up and down Lance's leg from hip to knee.

And smiled when he grumbled.

Letting my hand trail over his leg again, I gave my ass a tiny push backward.

And found his rock-hard cock.

My gasp echoed loudly in the silent shed, the only other sounds the soft breeze, frogs, and crickets playing a medley in the dark orchard.

Gripping his ass, I pulled him forward, our bodies fitting together perfectly.

"You're playin' with fire," Lance growled.

"If fire means you're going to give me that dick, I'm down."

Lance gripped my chest and pressed a kiss to my shoulder. "I don't have any condoms with me."

Shit.

"Me neither."

He nibbled gently on my neck, licking over the stinging spot.

"I haven't been with anyone in nearly a year before you, definitely nothing since my last test. Negative." His hot words hung heavy and hopeful at my ear.

"I haven't been with anyone since before you came to town," I offered. "And my last test was negative." The boa constrictor around my heart made it hard to breathe.

"Lube?" Lance teased a nipple with the flat of his thumb. "I'm not really a fan of the spit method."

"There's Vaseline in the first-aid kit."

He trailed his hand down my abs and brushed his knuckles over the length of my dick. "This means something to me," Lance whispered. "*You* mean something to me." He stroked my cock and thumbed through the pre-cum.

"Fuck, Lance," I whimpered.

He shifted to cup my balls, my breath hitching when he squeezed gently. With a soft push to the back of my thigh, he positioned my bent leg on the mattress. Pressing kisses down the center of my back, he stopped to nuzzle his nose between the two dimples of my lower back right above my ass.

"Don't move," he whispered before rolling from the bed and rummaging through the first-aid kit like a man on a mission.

He was back before my skin had time to cool, pressing his warmth against me and kissing the sensitive spot where my neck met my shoulder.

"Open it," he said as he handed me the Vaseline.

Once I'd worked the lid off, he dipped in two fingers.

The jelly was cool when his fingers worked between my ass cheeks, and I moaned.

"When I take you like this..." His words were gravel over sandpaper. "You're mine. You belong to me. This pretty little hole is gonna take my bare cock and there's no going back from that. This is real, Hudson. Do you understand me?"

A strangled cry escaped my lips.

"Forever, Hudson." Lance gripped my chin, his words stealing my breath. "Say it."

"Lance," I sobbed as he pressed first one and then another finger into my ass. "Please, give it to me."

"Not yet, sweetheart," Lance soothed at my ear as his slick fingers stretched and teased. "I need to hear it, need to know you understand this is forever. My bare cock deep in your ass, my load burning you up, marking you with my cum."

I gripped the base of my cock and squeezed to hold off the orgasm. "Forever, Lance. Oh god, give it to me."

His slick fingers slid from my ass, replaced by the thick head of his cock. Desire hung so heavy on the air I struggled to take my next breath. I cried out as Lance pressed into me, my tight ring giving way to the invasion.

"Fuck, Hudson," Lance panted, his hips rocking into me. "God, so tight. So fuckin' good."

We fell into a hard and fast rhythm, our bodies slapping together creating the perfect background noise. Sweat ran down my temple and the scent of sex hung heavy in the air. Lance's grunts against my ear matched my own labored breathing.

"Come for me," he demanded, his hand cupping my balls and teasing my taint.

"I'm so close," I whined.

"Wanna feel your ass tight around me when you come," Lance growled, never once losing the rhythm. "Fuck. Gonna give you my load, paint you with my cum."

His words sent me over the edge, and I exploded, making a mess of my fist and the bed. My ass clenched around Lance's thick cock, and he groaned. Burying his head in the crook of my neck he took my skin between his teeth. With a final thrust, he froze, grunting as he emptied himself into my ass.

Tiny aftershocks rocked through us as the shed glowed softly in the early morning sunlight.

His arms like vice grips around me, Lance kissed the spot where he bit me. "That wasn't just sex talk," he whispered. "I meant it. Forever, Hudson. I can't go back from what we just shared."

For several heartbeats, I said nothing.

But then I croaked out, "But what does that mean?"

He gripped my chin and turned my head for a kiss. "It means I'm head over heels in love with you and I'm not going anywhere. You own me."

"I..." The words lodged in my throat.

"You don't have to say anything right now. Let's sleep, clean up, and get home. The main thing you need to understand is I'm in this for good."

All I could do was nod.

Chapter 12

Lance

THE DAY WAS WARMING UP WHEN WE WOKE again.

Part of me wanted to stay cuddled in that cramped bed with Hudson forever.

But we had businesses to run and lives to live, plus, I'd hopefully made it clear that this wasn't something I was walking away from.

That damn little shed would forever hold a place in my heart.

We cleaned ourselves the best we could, dressed in our mostly dry, stiff clothing, and headed home.

At the door to Hudson's old farmhouse, I kissed him long and slow. Longing to hear him tell me he loved me, but knowing he had to come to it in his own time, I poured everything into that kiss.

"Come over later?" Hudson murmured against my lips.

I nodded. "Try to keep me away."

His cheeks pinked. "Bring a bag."

With my lip between my teeth, I nodded again. "See you in a bit."

A couple hours later, I'd checked in at the Sweet & Creamy, showered, and packed a bag. I thought about swinging by the roadhouse to see Henry but figured Hudson and I might end up there later anyway.

"I was gonna go walk the orchard, you wanna come with?" Hudson asked after an impromptu make-out session in his kitchen when I told him his shampoo smelled like apples and that was blasphemous for a peach orchard owner.

We walked every single row of trees while Hudson dictated notes into his phone. The crop looked good. He'd save a lot of peaches from the storm. And early numbers looked like the Riggs family would be in the black this season.

By the time we got back to his house, I was starving. "Let's go see Henry and get dinner."

"Like a date?" Hudson asked, his eyes bright and teasing.

"Yes, I'd like to take my boyfriend out on a date." I gripped him around the neck and pulled him in for a hard and fast kiss. "You got a problem with that?"

He smiled against my lips. "Mmm, who's this boyfriend of yours? I think I'd like to meet him."

I chuckled and slapped a palm against his ass, pulling him close so the soft swells behind our zippers pressed together. "He's an absolute pain in my ass. Running around orchards in storms. Doesn't know the meaning of the word *relax*. But he's gorgeous; an absolute Golden Retriever with the very best heart."

"Kinda sounds like you love him," Hudson whispered.

"I do." I cupped his face and kissed him softly. "Kinda hopin' if I show him I'm here for good, he'll figure out how to love me back one day."

A strangled sob escaped Hudson's chest and he kissed me fiercely. "He's a lucky guy to have someone like you."

"I'm the lucky one. He's the best thing that's ever happened to me and I plan to spend the rest of my life proving that to him."

Hudson shook his head. "You don't have to prove anything to me, Lance." He swallowed thickly. "I've never trusted anyone the way I trust you." He brought those beautiful blue eyes to mine. "Never thought I could trust enough to love someone, but then you came home and my whole world changed."

With our foreheads pressed together, we stood there, silently sharing the same air with each breath. "My heart never left Haven Grove. Just took coming home to figure out I loved you in a whole 'nother way than way back then."

"I love you," Hudson choked out. "It scares the ever-lovin' shit out of me, but I love you, Lance."

Tears stung my eyes, and I dotted kisses all over his face. "Forever, Hudson. I wasn't lyin' when I said I'm in this forever."

He shook his head. "I may suck at this; I don't have a single clue how to be someone's boyfriend."

"We'll figure it out together," I said, wrapping him in a hug.

We held each other for several heartbeats before I groaned.

"What?"

"Casey Joe is gonna fuckin' kill me."

Hudson chuckled, wiping his eyes and sniffling. "We'll break it to him easy. Let him know it's not just fuckin' around."

"Come on, let's go see Henry. Might as well get a good meal before your dad cuts off my dick and feeds it to his dog."

Hudson put me in a headlock. "He doesn't have a dog. And let's get back here quickly."

I wrestled my way out of his hold. "Why?"

"Because I need as much of that dick as I can get before it's gone," Hudson teased.

We were still laughing when we walked into the roadhouse.

Henry was behind the bar as usual, but the frown on his face wasn't his normal grumbly frown. He seemed lost in thought. When he finally looked up and caught sight of us, he brightened and waved us over.

"You finally talk my baby brother into a date?" Henry asked.

"I did. Date *and* boyfriend all at once," I said, throwing my arm around Hudson's shoulders.

"Damn, boy," Henry said. "When you go in, you go all in."

Hudson's flush was pretty in the dim light. "Yeah, well." He shrugged.

Henry whistled.

"Yeah, I know," I said.

"Been good knowing you," he said, sticking out his hand to shake.

I slapped his hand away. "We'll figure it out. Two beers and two of the specials."

Henry laughed. "Gotcha. It'll be right up."

He was still laughing as he pulled our beers from the tap and hollered to the kitchen to plate up two specials. Hudson and I settled at the far end of the bar where we could talk and watch people come and go.

When Henry brought our food and replaced our beers, he slung the towel over his shoulder and propped himself against the edge of the bar. "The trees okay?"

Hudson nodded. "Yeah, luckily the hail wasn't huge. Even more reason to get the rest of that netting rigged up. Saved a lot of the fruit."

Henry gave a small nod.

"Someone still sleeping out back?" I asked.

Henry wrinkled his brow. "Yeah."

"Nothing missing?"

He shook his head.

When he didn't go on, Hudson and I continued eating and Henry lumbered away. I'd known the guy long enough to know he was worried but hadn't figured out exactly how to handle the situation just yet.

"He's worried," Hudson said.

"Yep."

"He'll figure it out."

"Yep."

"My boyfriend, a man of such eloquent speech," Hudson teased.

I elbowed him. "I'll show you eloquent."

Hudson laughed, but then sobered, his eyes on someone at the door.

"What's wrong?"

"Just figure maybe we should make sure we tell Dad before anyone in town gets to him first."

"Good call. What about tomorrow night? It's my usual night to have pizza and beer with him. We could both go over?" My stomach soured at the thought of pissing Casey Joe off—honestly, I wouldn't even be able to blame him for being mad.

"You think plying him with pizza and beer every week is the best thing for his health?" Hudson asked with twin worry lines between his brows.

"I get light beer and he hasn't figured out the pizza has a cauliflower crust. My next step is sneaking some broccoli into the toppings." I shrugged and took a swallow of beer. "Figure he's gonna get the beer and pizza either way, this way it's halfway healthy. Not sure how to get rid of the smokes."

Hudson laughed. "Well, maybe tomorrow night you can take them away before he chops off your dick."

"Very funny." We could laugh, but I really had no clue how Casey Joe was going to take the news of Hudson and me together. Maybe getting him to stop smoking would need to wait until another time.

I needed Casey Joe to understand I'd gone and fallen in love with his son. Yeah, I was fucking Hudson, but it was so much more than that, and I needed my best friend to understand that. This wasn't a hookup. It wasn't random and temporary.

I needed him to know I'd spend the rest of my life loving and cherishing Hudson. But before we dropped our bomb, I wanted to make sure Hudson believed me.

Because *he* was the one who counted.

Hudson needed to know.

Needed to *never* fear me leaving.

As we settled up the bill—Henry never charging and me always leaving a chunk of bills on the bar—I checked my phone to make sure I had what I needed. Once we were outside in the dusk of evening, I pointed my chin toward the orchard.

"Wanna walk off dinner?" I asked.

Hudson nodded and I secretly sighed in relief that he never turned down the chance to be in the orchard.

When we reached the tree line, I took his hand. He looked at our entwined fingers and smiled. "Shit I never thought I needed or wanted," he muttered.

"Yeah well, you're stuck with them now."

As we rounded one row, Hudson gasped. "Oh my god, I didn't know it was a full moon." A large orange globe hung on the horizon.

"Looks just like a peach," I said. Pulling out my phone, I threw my arm around him and positioned the camera to capture us with the moon in the background. Then I kissed his cheek and took another shot.

When Hudson turned his head, our lips meeting in a sweet, hot kiss, I clicked another picture before pocketing my phone and pulling him into a full-body embrace. He tasted of beer, steak sauce, and ranch.

And he was mine.

I was the luckiest bastard alive to spend the rest of my life loving this man.

We finally broke apart and I guided our wandering toward the middle of the trees. Earlier in the day, I'd made a quick trip to the orchard and stacked three bushel baskets near a tree in hopes we'd make it out there after dinner.

"What the hell," Hudson muttered when he saw the baskets.

I pulled the song up on my phone and turned it up as loud as it would go.

When the very first notes rang out in the silent orchard, Hudson whipped to face me. I smiled, placed my phone on the stack of baskets, and held out my hand.

His chest heaved and for a split second I thought he'd refuse, but Hudson let me pull him close as Savage Garden's "I Knew I Loved You" played.

"Goin' a bit old school on this one," Hudson mumbled into my neck.

"Don't act like you don't know this song," I teased. "You're not *that* young."

"It's a good song."

We listened to the lyrics as we swayed in the soft breeze, the heavy scent of grass and peaches decorating the air.

"Thank you," Hudson whispered as the song started over.

"For what?"

"For giving me the chance to fall in love under the moonlight in the peach orchard." He rested his head on my shoulder. "I thought they'd ruined that for me, but you gave it back."

"What made you change your mind?" I asked.

Hudson snorted. "Like you gave me any choice?"

I pulled back and cupped his face. "You always have a choice."

He shook his head. "I think it was just you being you. Having you back in my life and realizing how much you meant to me. My heart hurt for so long—all I've ever wanted to do was protect it. But that pain helped me see how good love can be. Like being hurt made it easier to see when I had something real right in front of me. Doesn't mean I figured it out very quickly. And I still have no idea how to do a real relationship." He pressed a kiss to my lips. "But I also don't know how to be without you." Hudson frowned. "No, that's not true. I know how to be without you. I did it for eight years. It's just," he paused, swallowing, and meeting my gaze, "having you back made me see how much I need you in my life."

We danced through one more repeat before wandering back to Hudson's place hand-in-hand under the moonlight.

Making out in his kitchen led to two big guys squeezing into his shower.

"Damn ol' farmhouse bathroom," Hudson muttered. "Maybe I'll remodel."

Turning off the water, I handed him a towel. "It served its purpose."

He cocked a brow.

"It got us clean," I said. Grabbing his flushed, wet body I pulled him close. "And now we can get dirty all over again."

Round one started with great intentions, but mutual blow jobs later we chuckled sleepily and admitted defeat.

"Sleep first, then dirty," Hudson mumbled into my chest as I pulled the soft quilt up to our waists.

Pressing a kiss to his temple, I breathed him in and smiled.

When I woke, pale morning light streamed through the windows and Hudson grinned down at me from where he straddled my thighs. His hands gripped my chest, and he rocked his hips, the delicious friction between our cocks bringing me fully awake.

"Good morning," I croaked.

"Good morning."

"We have time?" I knew he was opening the store today since Wanda needed to take her mother to a doctor's appointment.

"For us? Always."

Swallowing thickly, I reached for the lube. "Get on your back and spread your legs for me."

Hudson's pretty little groan of pleasure was music to my ears as he rolled off me. Kneeling between his legs as I slicked my cock, his dick plump and smearing pre-cum against his belly, I sent up a prayer of thanks to anyone listening for bringing the two of us together again.

"Lift up," I demanded in the quiet room, shoving a pillow under his hips when he complied. Working a lube-covered finger into his ass, loving the way he gasped and rolled his hips, I kept my eyes glued to him while stretching his hole. Two fingers had him moaning, and when he begged for my cock, I knew I'd never be able to deny this man anything he asked for.

Lining my throbbing cockhead up with his hole, I inched into him. His grunts and whimpers danced on the air as the early morning sunshine washed the room in orange and pink. Exquisite tight heat welcomed me into his body, and I groaned when my balls pressed against him. Dropping to my elbows, bringing us chest to chest, I anchored my arms under him and gripped his shoulders.

"I love you," I whispered against his lips, pulling out and gliding back into him in one long, slow thrust.

Hudson let out a sob and wrapped his legs around my waist. "Fuck, Lance. Fuck." He cried out when I pulled out and thrust in again. "Oh god. Fuck. Love you. So fucking much."

We lost ourselves in our lovemaking as Haven Grove came alive that morning. Sweat-slicked bodies, soft, dirty words, and fingers entwined on faded blue sheets would forever be my favorite way to welcome in the day with Hudson.

His fingers dug into my ass, urging me to thrust faster and harder as ragged breaths ripped from his chest. "Please, Lance. Fuck. Please. So close."

Devouring his mouth, our tongues writhing together as I pumped into him, I gripped his shoulders and increased my speed. He exploded between us, the friction of our bodies bringing on his release, and I groaned into his mouth. Each pulse of his orgasm tightened his hole around me, driving me toward my own.

With a final thrust, I froze and buried my face in his neck as my hot, thick load spilled into him. Loving the way Hudson whimpered with each pulse of my dick, I sucked on his collarbone and rolled my hips, pushing my throbbing cock deeper.

When I could finally breathe almost normally, I slid

gently from his ass and gathered him in my arms. Kissing the back of his neck, chuckling as he squirmed when I hit a sensitive spot, I silently counted five more minutes before we had to get up and face the day.

The boots on the front porch didn't register at first.

Even when the knock sounded at the screen door, my brain wasn't worried.

The old door squeaked open and slammed shut and Casey Joe called out, "Hudson? You okay?"

Then, I panicked.

My body froze.

My brain sounded alarm bells, but the rest of me couldn't move. I lay there with Hudson in my arms doing nothing.

As if his *dad* wasn't about to find us blissed out and smelling of sex.

Like my best friend wasn't going to find me soaked in sweat and cum after thoroughly dicking down his baby boy.

Arguments of *He's a grown man* and *This is between the two of you* flew out the window as Casey Joe's heavy boots made their way to Hudson's room.

"Hudson?" he yelled again. "Everything okay? Thought I heard—"

Time stood still.

I was a dead man.

Chapter 13
Hudson

I LIKE TO THINK OF MYSELF AS PRETTY RELIABLE in a tense situation.

Quick thinker.

A spring into action type guy.

But my dad stood in the doorway to my bedroom, and I stared at him as if trying to solve the world's most difficult puzzle.

Luckily, Dad seemed to be having just as much difficulty comprehending the scene before him.

He blinked.

Opened his mouth.

Blinked again.

"Dad," I started as if his best friend wasn't plastered to me with sweat and cum.

"Case," Lance croaked.

"Get your asses out of bed and someone better be ready to tell me what the fuck is goin' on," Dad said, his face flushed, and words laced with a fiery anger. "I'll be on the porch."

"Shit." Lance pressed his forehead to my shoulder.

"Well, there goes the idea of easing him into it," I muttered.

We rolled from bed and took the world's fastest shower.

By the time we made our way to the kitchen, Dad had started a pot of coffee, and I could see him pacing on the front porch. Lance and I poured ourselves fortifying mugs of coffee and headed out the door.

Years of knowing each other was likely the only thing that kept Dad's blow to Lance's face from landing right on his nose. Instead, just as the punch flew through the air, Lance jerked to the side.

He cursed when Dad's fist glanced his cheek.

The coffee mug shattered on the porch, steaming black liquid splattering everywhere.

"Dad!" I stepped in front of him and put a hand on his chest. "Knock it off. We need to talk."

"What the hell you doin', Lance? Takin' advantage of my son? What the fuck?" Dad roared.

"Case—"

The second swing missed completely, and Dad stumbled.

"Dad, stop." I muscled him toward the porch swing. "Sit down."

"I trusted you." Dad's breaths heaved from his chest and his hand shook as he pointed a finger at Lance. "Trusted you to take care of my boys and this is what you do?"

"Case—" Lance started.

"No," I interrupted. "Dad, stop now. This has nothing to do with trust. You and I both know damn well Lance never hurt Henry and me. I'm a grown-ass man and I can make my own decisions."

Dad scoffed, rubbing his knuckles where he'd made decent contact with the side of Lance's face. "So now you're just fuckin' around? Scratchin' an itch? Fuck, didn't even know you were gay," he added almost as an afterthought.

"It's not just fuckin' around," Lance said. "And I didn't *know* I was gay until I left here, and things got worse with Kim." He moved closer to me.

"Well, you're in for shit," Dad muttered. "Hudson doesn't do anything but fuckin' around. She fuckin' screwed my boys up just as much as she fucked me over."

Lance stiffened beside me, and I knew without a doubt he was fixin' to defend my honor. I took his hand and a deep breath. "She did fuck me up," I said, letting Lance pull me closer as we faced Dad. "But I've been figuring some shit out lately. We're not just fuckin' around. This is real. We planned to tell you in a better way than this, but that's water under the bridge now."

"He's my *kid*," Dad roared, fiery eyes glaring at Lance.

"I know," Lance answered softly. "Didn't come here lookin' to fall in love with him." He turned soft eyes my way. "But I don't regret it. He's the best thing that ever happened to me."

Dad stood, opened his mouth, shut it, and balled his hands into fists. "Thought I knew you. Trusted you.

Should've known everyone's gonna fuck me over in the end." He made his way down the porch steps.

"Dad," I called out, unsure if I wanted him to come back or keep walking.

He waved a hand in the air, never turning back.

"Fuck," Lance grumbled.

"Well, that could have gone better."

We spent the rest of the day working through chores and to-do lists at the Dairy Palace, the Juicy Peach, and around the orchard. Things got done, but I could honestly say neither of us was focused on the work.

We chatted throughout the day, mostly about Dad, and had come to the conclusion that we'd give him a day or so to cool off, and then go talk to him. I wasn't willing to lose my dad over this.

And Lance wasn't going to let his best friend go without a fight.

Hopefully, he just needed time.

"You wanna get food or cook something at the house?" I asked. Maybe assuming he'd spend the night with me again was crossing a line, but after the morning with Dad, I couldn't help feeling needier than usual.

"Kinda don't want Henry's scrutiny and told-you-so's tonight," Lance said. "Pizza?"

"That sounds perfect," I answered as we walked through the back door into the kitchen.

"You wanna shower and I'll put in the order?" Lance asked as he thumbed his phone screen.

"Thanks." I pressed a kiss to his lips. Despite Dad catching us together, I refused to feel like a teen who'd gotten in trouble. I wasn't going to feel guilty for what Lance and I had, even if Dad couldn't wrap his head around it.

Stripping my shirt over my head as I headed toward the bathroom, Lance's phone chimed and I heard him curse. Right before I turned on the water, his rich voice filled the air as he answered the call.

Just as I'd unbuttoned my jeans, Lance appeared in the bathroom doorway. "Get dressed. We need to go."

"Huh?"

"Casey Joe. Henry said he thinks he's having a heart attack. Henry's got him almost to the hospital, couldn't wait on the ambulance."

The bottom dropped out of my world.

I froze.

Lance kicked into action. Buttoning my jeans, scooping my shirt off the floor, and pulling it over my head. He cupped my cheek, kissed me softly, and pulled me into a quick hug. "Come on, we need to go. We need to be there for him."

Silently, I followed Lance to his truck.

We'd been driving a few minutes when the dam broke and tears stung my eyes. "Fuck, what if that fight is the last memory we have of him."

"Shhh," Lance said, taking my hand and bringing my knuckles to his lips for a kiss. "We'll get there."

"This is my fault," I started.

"No. We're not playing that game."

"He had a *heart attack* the day he found us in bed together," I rushed out in exasperation.

"He had a heart attack because he's been on the brink of something happening ever since Billy died and probably before." Lance squeezed my hand. "And we don't even know if it's a heart attack."

My mind rushed with memories of my dad and how much I'd miss him if he was gone. He wouldn't be winning any Parent of the Year awards, but he'd done the best he could with what he had. I wasn't ready to see him go. Hell, we still needed to have it out over Lance and me.

"Fuck," I muttered. "This is so much shit." Rubbing my eyes, I tried not to imagine a doctor coming out to tell Henry and me that our dad didn't make it.

Fuck.

He had to make it.

Lance held my hand all the way to the hospital. "You go on in. I'll park." He pulled up to the Emergency Department doors.

My brain knew I needed to get out of the damn truck, but I was frozen. What if I walked in there and Henry told me Dad was dead?

What if a nurse looked at me with sympathy and shook her head sadly?

Was he in there right now with monitors beeping and alarms buzzing as his heart failed?

Was he dying? Already dead?

Lance leaned in and gripped my neck. "Hudson. Go see your dad. I'll be in as soon as I park. You need to be in there—you and Henry, you've got this, and I'll be right there." His kiss filled me with courage and hope. "I love you. No matter what happens, we'll get through this."

Swallowing a lump in my throat, I nodded and gave his hand a squeeze. "Love you," I managed to croak out.

Then I slid from the truck and made my way toward the sliding doors.

Chapter 14
Lance

WITH MY HEART IN MY THROAT AND MY PULSE galloping like the pony express, I made my way from the far end of the parking lot toward the Emergency Department doors.

Hudson needed me. He was strong and he'd make it through no matter what, but I couldn't fathom leaving him to deal with this on his own. Especially not when he was feeling vulnerable after Casey walked in on us.

Fuck.

The fight seemed a thousand miles away.

But the throbbing bruise on my cheekbone was enough to remind me it was just that morning.

Had finding me with Hudson triggered my best friend's heart attack?

Fuck.

I told Hudson we weren't going to play the blame game, so I needed to focus on something else.

The doors slid open, and a blast of cold, antiseptic-heavy air assaulted me.

To my left was the registration desk. Straight ahead were swinging doors. And to my right—

"Lance," Henry called out.

Hudson sat slouched in a chair, his head in his hands.

Henry slapped me on the back and motioned for me to sit on the little bench with Hudson. The moment I joined him, Hudson shifted into me. My hand went to his leg, and I squeezed.

"What do you know?" I asked.

Henry shrugged. "Dad came by the bar after he—" He cleared his throat and gestured toward us. "Ranting and raving about trust and sneaking behind his back and playing him for the fool."

Hudson huffed and ran hands through his hair.

"Anyway, he downed a beer and went home. Later, he texted me and wanted to know what was wrong with my beer because he felt like shit. Said he wanted to nap because he was exhausted and lightheaded, but his stomach hurt, and he couldn't get a good breath." Henry shook his head. "I got someone to cover and headed over there. He was sweaty and pale and kept saying it felt like someone was gripping his heart. I ignored his bitching and made him get in the truck. He complained the whole way here, but I think it was mostly out of fear. It's not like he doesn't know he's been on a downhill swing for quite a while. He was alert and answering questions when they took him back. Nurse said they'd do some tests and let us know what's going on."

"If you need to head back," Hudson started.

"No, I'm good." Henry didn't leave the bar for much, so it was clear he was concerned for his dad.

We sat silently for a bit as the sounds of the ER filtered through the air around us.

"This isn't your fault," Henry said, his words low and firm as he clasped Hudson's shoulder. "He was heading toward an issue all on his own."

"He was really upset," Hudson said. "He punched Lance."

Henry winced and spared a glance toward my cheek.

"People are upset every day. Punches get thrown all the time. Those things don't bring on heart attacks. If they did, we'd have a lot more people dying."

A young man in scrubs came through the door and headed our way, his approach stirring the apprehension around us.

"With Casey Riggs?" His nametag said Craig.

The three of us stood.

Craig looked a bit surprised to be surrounded by three men towering over him like trees, but he kept his composure. "Vitals are stable for now. We've got him on a heart monitor and ran an EKG. We're waiting on his chest x-ray to come back, and the lab is running his bloodwork now."

"What does that mean?" Henry asked.

Craig gave a soft smile. "It means that nothing is conclusive yet, but based on symptoms and initial tests, Mr. Riggs did have a heart attack."

Hudson huffed and crossed his arms. "Is he awake?"

"He's sedated enough to keep him comfortable, but he's been able to answer our questions."

"What are the next steps?" I asked.

"Once we have his bloodwork, we'll know more, but likely a cardiac catheterization with possible stent deployment in the cath lab. Then he's looking at being here for a few days."

"Can we see him?" Hudson asked.

"We can let one person go back but only briefly. The ER is extremely busy right now and there's not enough room for visitors," Craig explained. "Once he's done in the cath lab, he'll be on the fourth floor for monitoring. You'll be able to see him for a short time once he's settled, but visiting hours tomorrow will be open."

Hudson gritted his teeth. "You go," he told Henry. "Let him know we're here and we'll see him once he's upstairs."

For a moment, I thought Henry would object, but he just nodded and turned to follow Craig.

"I'm sure he doesn't want to see me," Hudson mumbled.

"Hey," I said, gripping his arm. "Casey Joe loves his family and he'll be grateful you're here." My best friend had been through a lot of shit and his attitude had shown the wear and tear, but there was never a doubt in my mind how much his boys meant to him.

The ER waiting room was full of patients standing around in various states of distress. No place we needed to hang out.

"Let's get out of here. They're going to move him, so we don't need to be here."

Hudson followed me silently out the sliding doors.

"We'll get some food at the cafeteria and pick

something up for Henry. I think they have a nice little patio area outside of the cafeteria. We can sit there until we hear from him."

We headed toward my truck. Hudson's shaky breath when he settled next to me hurt my heart. Without a word, I reached for him and pulled him close. His sob reverberated through me and hung thick on the air inside the cab.

I let him cry, glad he was comfortable enough with me to let it out.

Hudson's breathing eventually evened out, and he sighed. "Sorry—"

Cutting him off, I gripped his chin and brought his face up to mine. "Don't you ever apologize for having feelings and sharing them with me."

Hudson's stomach growled. "Guess food would be good," he said with a chuckle.

I pointed the truck toward the main entrance.

"It's good he's awake and talking," Hudson mused as I circled the lot. "I'm sure he'll be bitching about the food and asking to go home soon enough."

"The nurses will probably draw straws for who has to deal with him," I agreed.

"Maybe this will be a turning point for him. That push he needed to get beyond Billy and Mom and take his life back."

The hopefulness in Hudson's words buoyed me. "Let's hope."

Once inside the hospital, we easily found the cafeteria. Henry texted while we waited in line.

Henry: He's in the cath lab now. They said 4th floor in a couple hours. Where are you?

Me: Cafeteria. You want anything?

Henry: Yeah, just whatever.

Me: Gonna sit on the cafeteria patio.

Henry: Ok

We skipped the dinner options of Salisbury steak, grilled chicken, and lasagna, and grabbed deli sandwiches, chips, and drinks. Hudson grinned and gave me a thumbs up when he saw the dessert options included peach crumble and ice cream from The Juicy Peach and Dairy Palace.

Henry already had a table for us on the patio near one of the outdoor heaters. Summer was in full swing, but the evening breeze had cooled things down considerably.

"How is he?" Hudson asked.

"Good. Subdued," Henry said as he took a bite of his sandwich. "Not sure if that's the drugs or just being tired. He asked about you guys. Wanted to know if you were coming to see him."

Hudson perked up. "That's good, right? If he's asking for us maybe it means he's not written us off for good."

Henry scowled. "He was taken off guard. Last time he found someone he loved in bed with another person he loved, it tore his life apart."

"Fuck," Hudson mumbled. "Hadn't thought about that."

I took Hudson's hand. "Hindsight's twenty-twenty, but we maybe should have told him sooner."

Hudson huffed. "We were telling him over pizza and beer tonight. That was the plan. It wasn't like either of us knew he'd come walking into my bedroom."

We ate in silence until Henry cleared his throat. "We'll see him settled into his room and then head home. Tomorrow, we can take turns sitting with him during visiting hours. Once we know how long he'll be here, we can figure out shifts. Depending on when he goes home and how he's doing, we may want to look at getting someone to come to the house."

Hudson scowled. "We're all right nearby, we can check on him."

Henry didn't look convinced. "We can check on him, and we will, but I was thinking more along the lines of someone to make sure he's got some healthy meals. Get him up and doing some exercises. There's got to be someone who could do that."

"Probably ask one of the nurses, they may know a company that provides that kind of service," I said.

Hudson nodded. "I guess he'd probably take that kind of thing better from someone else than one of us."

Henry finished his food and checked his phone. "Gonna move my truck. I'll see you up on the fourth floor."

Hudson and I gathered our trash and started wandering toward the elevators. Once on the fourth floor, we noticed the large picture window with a view of the sunset and Haven Grove toward the west.

Taking his hand, I gave it a squeeze. Hudson gripped me like I was a lifeline.

"Hey," I started. "He's awake and alert, they're fixing him up. He's not gone. We're gonna get through this."

Henry exited the elevator and fell into step beside us.

Casey Joe was pale and looked tiny in the hospital bed. Wires trailed from all parts of him, and the oxygen cannula seemed to take up his whole face.

But he was telling a nurse he wasn't going to stay in the hospital more than a day or two when we walked in. The older nurse huffed and said he'd have to prove he was ready to go home and get himself back in better health if he thought he was leaving on *his* timeline.

She winked at us as she bustled to the corner to type on a computer. "These must be the sons. Mr. Riggs has given permission for you to know his medical information. The doctor can answer more questions for you tomorrow, but he's had a heart catheterization and a stent deployment. We expect him here for monitoring for two or three days."

Casey Joe yanked back the curtain as she spoke. He caught sight of us and scowled. "Well, drag your sorry asses over here."

Hudson made his way to the far side of Casey's bed and pulled up a chair.

I followed suit.

Henry moved to stand behind us.

"Don't suppose I could ask the Judas to leave," Casey Joe drawled.

"Dad," Hudson warned.

Henry cleared his throat.

"Just not sure I've got much to say to him right now." Casey's eyes flicked my way, but he looked away quickly.

"If you ask him to leave, I go with him," Hudson said, his voice pained but strong.

Casey Joe yanked off the oxygen and rubbed at his nose as he glanced between the two of us. Eventually, he huffed and stuck the prongs back up his nose. "Whatever. Visiting time is almost over."

"We're gonna take turns sitting with you until you're out of here," I said.

"Don't need a damn babysitter," Casey muttered.

"Then it's good we're family," Hudson said with a challenging grin.

"Guess this means I have to stop smoking," my best friend griped.

"Probably for the best," I agreed.

"Fuck."

"Maybe listen to what the doctors say about improving your diet," Henry said.

"Next thing you'll be telling me to stop drinkin'," Casey griped.

"Let's commit to light beer as a starting point," I offered.

Casey shot me a look and rolled his eyes. "Not drinkin' with a backstabber."

Hudson stood up. "Dad, that's enough. We'll be back tomorrow. Don't give the nurses a hard time, they're here to help and get you home sooner rather than later."

"You can come alone," Casey Joe mumbled, exhaustion settling over his features.

"You want me here?" Hudson asked.

"'Course I want my kid here."

"Then *we* will be here."

Casey Joe glared at me, his eyes softening when he glanced at Hudson who stood with his arms crossed over his chest. Henry looming behind his brother, always the protector.

Casey grumbled and waved us away. "Go on, I'll see you tomorrow."

As we made toward the door, Casey Joe called out, "Lance."

Giving Hudson's hand a squeeze, I nodded toward the door and waited until he'd closed it behind him and Henry before walking to Casey's bedside.

"You love him?" he rasped out, the day and his condition definitely catching up to him.

"More than you could ever understand."

Casey worked his jaw. "Not feeling very understanding right now."

"I get that."

"So, you're gay?"

I hooked my thumbs in my jeans pockets and took a deep breath. "Not sure on a label that really works for me. Bi, pan, something else...but I fell hard for Hudson and we're really good together."

Casey's nostrils flared and it had nothing to do with the oxygen flowing through the cannula. "Think I'm done talkin' for tonight," he grumbled and pulled the sheet up to his chest. "Guess I'll see y'all tomorrow."

I placed a hand on his shoulder. "I'm really glad we're not saying goodbye to you. The boys need you."

He scoffed and I gave a squeeze.

"Maybe not the way they needed you way back then, but you three have always been a team even when the game wasn't going your way. They're grown and independent, but no one is ever ready to say goodbye to their parent. They need you to stick around; you all have some healing to do."

Casey's eyes shimmered as he covered my hand with his. "This doesn't mean I forgive you."

"I know."

"Doesn't mean I'm not gonna kick your ass when you least expect it."

"Understood."

He yawned. "Get out of here. I had a fuckin' heart attack and I need to rest."

Chuckling, I squeezed his shoulder once more and headed toward the door.

Hudson turned worried eyes my way when I found him alone in the hallway. "What did he say?"

I shrugged. "He asked if I loved you."

Hudson studied my face, waiting.

"I told him I loved you more than he'd ever understand."

Hudson's eyes softened and he bit his lip. "So, he's okay with things?"

I barked out a laugh. "Wouldn't say that. But I think we'll get there."

Chapter 15
Hudson

"How is he today?" I asked Henry when we met in the fourth floor waiting area.

Henry frowned. "Grumpier today. I think he was worn out last night, but today he's rested and feeling pretty decent. He's mad at the two of you. Mad that I didn't tell him about you guys. Mad that he's in the hospital. Mad that he had a heart attack." My brother ran a hand over his beard. "Mad is pretty much today's theme."

"Did you ask today's nurses if they know anyone who could check in, help with meals, get him exercising?" Lance asked.

Henry brightened. "Yeah, there's a nurse named Cassie. Her brother's name is Bryce. She said he's a certified personal trainer, but he's done that kind of thing before—checking in, healthy meals, light cleaning, exercise routine."

"But?" I asked.

Henry grimaced. "He's planning on moving to Haven

Grove soon, but he doesn't have a place just yet. So, if we hired him, he'd likely need to use the spare room at Dad's house. And he's not in a position to be here right away."

Lance whistled and I wrinkled my nose. "Yeah, I don't see that going over well."

"Maybe we can figure out a way to convince him," I said.

"Or we tell him this is the way it is," Lance put in.

Henry and I stared at him as if he'd grown two heads.

"What?" Lance shrugged. "He wants to get better? Wants to be around for his boys?"

"Wow, it's like you just want to get punched again," Henry deadpanned. "I need to get going. Here's a card for Bryce. I told Cassie to mention the situation to him and we'd likely get in touch. I'm on shift until close tonight, but I can do the early visit tomorrow."

I hugged my brother and then smiled as Henry gave Lance a hug and said goodbye.

Moving to stare out the huge picture window, I ran through possible scenarios with my dad.

"Hey," Lance whispered, his soft breath against my ear. "You don't have to go in—"

"No, I do. I want to see him. Want to make sure he knows we want him to get better."

"He's mad. He might say shitty things."

"I know."

"If it comes down to it...if he makes you choose between him and me—"

I whirled on Lance. "Fuck that. There's no choice. But there doesn't need to be. He'll either get over this or he won't. I'm not giving up on us just because his damn stubborn ass can't get past a lifetime of loss."

"He's hurt, Hudson. Give him some time."

"He found out yesterday that time isn't a given. I love him, love my family, but I love you too, and I won't give up one for the other." I gripped Lance's hand.

"Then let's get in there and visit his cranky ass," Lance said, leaning in to press a kiss to my cheek.

Dad was just as grumpy as Henry had described.

He hated the food. Hated the hospital gown. The doctors were assholes who didn't know a damn thing. The nurses got satisfaction from torturing him.

"Just want to be home in my own bed with decent channels." Dad ran a hand over his scruffy chin and balled his fists.

"These are the same channels you've got at home," Lance said as he clicked through the lineup.

Digging in my pocket, I pulled out a peppermint. "Here. You're going through nicotine withdrawal. Suck on this."

"Not gonna help the shakes or the headache," Dad groused as he popped it in his mouth.

"No, but it will give you something to do with your mouth." I glanced toward Lance. "Could you run downstairs and see if the gift shop has suckers? Maybe having something in his mouth and a stick to hold onto will help."

Lance nodded and gripped the back of my neck.

I wanted to melt into his arms and let him hold me. Wanted to lose myself in his kiss. But we were here for Dad.

"I'll be right back," Lance said with a gentle squeeze.

Dad scowled at his best friend's back.

He sat there scowling for several minutes while I wondered how to make things right between us.

A nurse bustled in and asked Dad if he wanted me to leave while she checked his vitals. He groused that he'd rather she leave, so she clucked her tongue with a grin and sped through her routine.

When she was gone, I stood at the edge of his bed and gripped the cold metal.

"I need you to know I love him." My soft words were barely loud enough to be heard. "We didn't mean for this to happen."

Dad scoffed. "He just happened to fall into your bed and end up with his dick in your ass?"

"Don't be crude," I shot back. "That's not all this is."

Dad huffed and rolled his eyes.

"I think I'd already fallen halfway before I even knew it was him. Then I saw him for the first time again and my world shifted—the draw between us didn't make sense. Hell, it shouldn't have made sense. But it was there, and it was strong.

"For a while, I thought I could play my usual game and be okay with letting him go, but I don't think I can ever let him go. I don't know how to make you understand it. I don't know how to make you okay with it. But he's it for me. We aren't going anywhere. I want you in my life. *We* want you in our lives. We want you around. He's your best friend, but he's my everything."

Dad's eyes shifted to the door, and he huffed. "Guess that little speech probably got him all lovey-dovey."

I turned to see Lance with a bag from the gift shop, his eyes so full of emotion my breath caught. His hand came to the small of my back and he pressed a kiss to my temple. "I love you so damn much," he murmured.

Dad took the bag of suckers from Lance with a scowl and a grumbled thank you. He tore into one of the wrappers and shoved it into his mouth, quickly molding his fingers around the stick like he used to hold a cigarette. "I'd kill for a big ol' fountain Coke. They've let me have hot tea for a bit of caffeine, but if I'm gonna feel like death without the smokes, the least someone could do is get me a Big Gulp."

I smiled, my blood flowing like hot lava as Lance's thumb rubbed my lower back. "We'll see what we can do when we come back tomorrow."

The sucker had calmed Dad a bit and he gave a nod. Popping the candy from his mouth, holding it just like he'd hold a smoke, he said, "You seen any of the shit Henry's dealing with at the roadhouse?"

Lance and I nodded. "Saw some of the trash mess."

"Needs to call the police."

"You know Henry's not gonna purposely get someone in trouble, especially if they aren't doing any real harm and he thinks they might be in a rough spot." My brother's heart was the best thing about him.

"Well, keep an eye out, yeah?" Dad said before popping the sucker back into his mouth.

"Will do," Lance said. "See you tomorrow." He patted Dad's shoulder, and I leaned in to hug him.

"Love you," I said. "Try not to be an asshole."

Dad mumbled something about seeing what he could do.

As we reached the door, he croaked out, "Hudson."

Lance and I both turned around.

"He might be my best friend, but you're my son."

I froze and Lance tensed beside me.

"Dad..." I started.

He gestured toward us with the sucker. "Since I'm not dying—not yet, anyway—I'll figure out some way to be okay with this."

My throat tightened as tears threatened, and Lance took my hand.

"We'd like that," I said.

Dad gave a nod and pointed the sucker our way. "Might have to kick his ass first."

Lance chuckled. "Bring it on. You get yourself back into shape enough to fight me, and you can give it your best go."

Chapter 16

Lance

WET HEAT ENGULFED MY DICK AS EARLY morning light painted the walls of Hudson's bedroom. "Fuck," I grunted, loving the swirl of Hudson's tongue around my shaft. Yanking him up, I caught his lips in a slow, bone-melting kiss. "Good morning," I murmured into his mouth.

"Morning." Hudson's grin and the scent of his sleep-rumpled skin were my own personal treasures. "We've got a shitload of things to do," he said, biting his lip and rocking his hard cock against my thigh, "but I thought we could start the day off right."

"Mmm, that's what you thought, huh?" I savored the slow, leisurely kiss.

We were having a barbeque at the Juicy Peach sponsored by the orchard, the roadhouse, and the Dairy Palace. A celebration of a bumper crop of peaches and bringing the townsfolk together.

Hudson and I had a lot to celebrate as well.

Once Casey Joe was released from the hospital, we'd gotten him settled in at his place. Of course, he'd refused the suggestion of any help and stubbornly claimed he'd do it himself because he wasn't an invalid. So, the three of us had taken to daily check-ins as he recovered.

For the first couple months, he'd done an okay job of taking better care of his health. But Hudson, Henry, and I had already noticed a slip in his determination. It was something we'd have to address with Casey soon, but we were waiting until his next checkup with the doctor.

Henry had his own little situation going on, but he'd been pretty tight-lipped about it. All I knew was he was preoccupied and maybe even a bit…was smitten the right word? Definitely distracted and knee-deep into whatever was going on. Hudson and I agreed we'd let Henry tell us about whatever was going on in his own time, but that didn't mean we weren't curious as hell.

Hudson and I had only been back from a short trip to the city for a few days, but we'd returned to Haven Grove ready to wrap up the summer and get a good start on everything fall-related for the orchard, store, and ice cream shop.

The trip to the city had been productive.

I'd signed the papers to finalize the sale of my ice cream shop there so I could turn right around and buy out my mom for the Dairy Palace.

Hudson, my sweet Golden Retriever of a man, had taken in the city with wide-eyed enthusiasm—loving the restaurants, theater shows, and five-star hotel—but declared he was a country boy at heart.

We'd both been happy to get back to our simpler life in Haven Grove.

Hudson whimpered into my mouth as I deepened the kiss.

I ran my hand down his back, savoring each hard line and soft curve. "Exactly what did you have in mind?"

Hudson grinned and gripped my dick. "Grab the lube and I'll show you."

Sex with Hudson was amazing, and I had no doubt we'd never get bored. Things were too electric and soul-deep between us. And it wasn't just the sex. What we had was so much more than could be described by words. Every day we got to spend together, getting to know each other in our new roles, and finding new reasons to fall head over heels in love reminded me exactly why my heart had never settled for being away from Haven Grove.

Hudson slicked his hole and tossed me the lube before positioning himself on his hands and knees, his legs spread for me as he stroked his cock. As I pressed my lubed dick to his pucker, Hudson's eyes shot toward the door.

Smoothing a hand down his back, I chuckled. "It's locked, all good."

And then we lost ourselves to the moment. The tight heat of his body opening for me. His gasp of pleasure as I stretched that taut ring of muscle. The perfect rhythm, the slide of my shaft in and out of his ass, the slap of sweaty skin, the hot press of our bodies.

Gripping Hudson's hips, loving the dig of my fingers into his soft flesh, I breathed in deeply savoring the scent of our lovemaking.

Falling.

Deeper.

Pouring myself into him as the soundtrack of our coupling danced on the air, our hearts and bodies becoming one; desperately straining for release.

Shifting forward, I pressed my chest to Hudson's back. Wrapping an arm around him, my hand gripping his chest, I whispered, "Love you. Love being inside you. Love being by your side. Love knowing you love me back."

Hudson's breaths came in great gulps, his hips rocking back to meet my thrusts. "Fuck, Lance. Holy fuck. God, it's so good. So fucking good."

With my arm still clutching him close, I straightened upright, bringing Hudson with me. The new position forced a cry from his lips, his arms reaching overhead to tangle his fists in my hair.

"God, Hudson. You are so fucking good. So tight and so perfect for me." I sucked on the sensitive skin where his neck met his shoulder as I pumped my hot, slick cock into the heat of his body. Reaching for his dick, I took him in my fist and stroked. "Wanna feel this tight ass on my cock when you come for me."

Hudson moaned and thrust his hips back and forth, sliding his cock into my fist and riding my dick. "Please, Lance. Fuck. Please. Give it to me."

With a gentle bite to his neck and a thumb teasing over his nipple, Hudson froze and cried out as his release spilled over my fingers. The hot clench of his ass had me grunting through my orgasm as I pumped my hot load into him.

Breathing like we'd run ten miles, we dropped to the mattress laughing through kisses and totally spent.

"Well, damn," Hudson drawled. "Now we're gonna have to cancel the barbeque since I won't be able to walk normal for a fuckin' week."

I chuckled and pressed a kiss to the swell of his bicep. "No can do, we've got that new roadhouse peach-infused barbeque sauce set to show off. Plus, the cinnamon peach whiskey and caramel peach ice cream. You'll just have to suck it up, buttercup."

We kissed and touched and laughed through a shower and getting ready for the day. While I hadn't officially moved into the old farmhouse, I spent much of my time there, and we'd fallen into a nice routine. The bathroom was small, but we moved together through showering, brushing our teeth, and combing our hair almost effortlessly.

Dressed in worn jeans, a dark gray t-shirt, and work boots, I started coffee while Hudson finished in the bathroom.

"Shit, are we out of eggs?" I asked as I bent to inspect the fridge.

"Should be some in the other one," Hudson said as he pulled bread from the package for toast.

Heading out to the mudroom to check for another dozen eggs, I caught sight of Casey Joe lounging in a chair under the big oak tree out back.

"Hudson?" I called out.

He appeared at the door to the mudroom looking fucking edible in light wash jeans, a teal t-shirt, and socked feet, his gaze following mine. "Well, shit."

"Invite him in for breakfast."

Hudson swung open the screen door. "Dad? What are you doing out here?"

Casey Joe startled at his son's voice and pulled himself from wherever his mind had taken him. "Thought I'd help if you needed it. Got any coffee?" His fingers gripped a sucker, and he popped it in his mouth as he walked toward the door.

I grabbed the eggs and slapped Casey Joe on the back as he walked into the house.

In the kitchen, he placed a wrapped box with a bow on the counter and popped the sucker from his mouth. "These damn things are gonna rot my teeth and give me diabetes," he groused. "Might as well just go back to cigarettes."

"The suckers smell better, and I doubt you'll die from a cavity or two," Hudson said as he got three mugs from the cabinet.

"Brush your teeth sometimes," I said, elbowing Casey as I headed toward the stove. "You'll be fine."

Hudson manned the toast while I scrambled eggs.

"You two heathens not even gonna cook up some bacon?" Casey Joe asked.

"You know where the skillet is," Hudson said over his shoulder, but I didn't miss the grin playing on his lips.

Casey Joe settled in next to me to fry bacon and the three of us worked in comfortable silence to put together a pretty damn tasty breakfast.

Once settled at the table with our food and coffee, Casey nodded toward the gift. "Open that later. Not even sure what it's for—guess to say good job for saving the orchard or something like that."

Hudson eyed me over his coffee cup, but neither of us said a word.

Casey Joe huffed. "And maybe kinda a way to say I'm sorry for walking in on you—fuck, won't ever make that mistake again—and I'm sorry for the way I reacted when I found out you were together. Took me by surprise— woulda seen a tsunami wiping out Haven Grove before I guessed about you two. But that damn heart attack made me see I'm glad to be here. Glad to have you all in my life." The words rushed from him before he took a long swig of coffee and returned to eating.

Hudson's hand found mine under the table and I gave a little squeeze.

I hadn't *known* my best friend would come around, but I'd wanted very badly to believe he would. He loved his son too much to let him go, even if that meant dealing with the fact I was now taking on a very different role in Hudson's life.

Breakfast was nice, though Casey Joe seemed distracted.

We cleaned up and Casey popped another sucker in his mouth. "Guess I'll see you at the Peach." He waved the sucker our way and headed out the back door.

"That was a bit weird," Hudson mumbled.

"He's trying. The health scare, the fact that he's not keeping up with things on his own, undiagnosed depression—" I paused when Hudson's brows shot up. "What? You don't think he's definitely got depression?"

Hudson shrugged. "Yeah, probably. Guess I'd just never really thought about it."

"Stopping by, cooking bacon, dropping off a gift, offering to help with today," I said, "it's all his way of reaching out the best he can right now. I'd say most days he's fighting just to keep his head above water."

"How do we fix that?" Hudson curled into me, letting me pull him close.

"I'm not sure we can. *He* has to be the one to realize he needs help and be ready to accept it. Maybe he's doing better than we think and he'll get a good report from the doctor."

"At least he stopped the cigarettes and beer."

"Most of the beer."

I pulled him in for a hug and kiss before we pulled the door closed behind us and headed out for an afternoon of fun with our favorite small town.

The barbeque turned out to be a great time. Most of the folks in Haven Grove either hadn't realized Hudson and I were a couple now, or they just didn't care. We spent the day talking, laughing, and sharing our goods with the town.

Henry's Roadhouse crew manned the food tables, dishing up BBQ pork, brisket, and sides. The peach-infused barbeque sauces were a huge hit and the limited number of cases we'd ordered were completely sold out by the end of the day.

Henry mixed cocktails like they were going out of style and couldn't wipe the grin from his face when person after person raved about the cinnamon peach whiskey along with his specialty mixed drinks.

The dessert table was a desolate wasteland by the time we wrapped things up, not even a crumb of caramel peach cobbler was to be found. Every other dessert had been gobbled up as well.

The Juicy Peach, Dairy Palace, and Riggs Family Roadhouse swag was absolutely wiped out, and my head was already calculating the reorders we'd need to tackle.

"Oh my god," Hudson groaned as we dropped onto the front porch swing after the barbeque. "We have so much inventory to go through and orders to make."

I laughed. "Exactly what I was thinking."

"Tomorrow," he said, resting his head on my shoulder. "Let's go watch the stars in the orchard."

We washed up and gathered a blanket, some fruit, and wine.

"Grab the gift," I suggested. Having absolutely no idea what Casey Joe might have opted to give us, I figured we might as well open it now rather than putting it off.

The moon shone brightly on the orchard. Rows of trees cast shadows along the ground. In an intersection of two pathways, Hudson spread out the blanket.

The night was warm, and we stripped out of our shirts before laying out on the blanket, our heads meeting in the middle while our bodies stretched in opposite directions. Our shoulders pressed together, and Hudson feathered a kiss to my arm before cupping my face and bringing our lips together.

"Today was good," he murmured against my lips.

"Any day we get to spend together, working and sharing our life is good." I deepened the kiss.

Hudson broke away, pressing his forehead to mine. "Let's open the gift."

I handed the box to him and smiled as he tore into it. Even now, Hudson had the enthusiasm of a puppy with a chew toy when it came to opening gifts.

Tossing the wrapping paper, box, and tissue paper to the side, Hudson pursed his lips and frowned at the folded rectangle of metal and wood. Covering his hand with mine, I gripped the knob and turned it, winding up what appeared to be a music box.

As the first strains of "Photograph" by Ed Sheeran tinkled from the music box, Hudson opened the two halves of the rectangle and whispered, "Oh my god."

"What?"

He turned a double photo frame my way. The moon wasn't the best light, but in the left-side frame, I could easily make out a picture of me and Hudson from about a week before I left Haven Grove. I sat on the tailgate of my old truck, laughing about something; probably some dumb-ass shit Casey Joe had said. Hudson stood behind me and to the side with his gangly arms pressed against the side of my truck; all smile, elbows, and a look of adoration painted on his face.

Swallowing a lump in my throat, I took Hudson's hand as he ran a finger over the two men behind the glass. "So much has changed," he murmured.

"But in some ways, nothing has," I whispered into the soft hair at his temple.

The photograph on the right had been taken about a week ago.

Me on the tailgate of my truck again. My legs dangling

and spread to make room for Hudson. His back pressed into my chest while he sat on the very edge of the tailgate. My arms wrapped around him, his hands on my wrists. We were both laughing, faces awash in sunlight, and that same look of adoration on Hudson's face as he tipped his head up to look at me.

But this time, my face mirrored his.

Adoration, respect, friendship, and love.

The picture frame held our history and our future.

Pain and healing.

Family and friendship.

A love from way back then and the same but different love of now.

And the love of forever.

"Well, Dad wins the best gift ever award," Hudson said with a sniffle.

I rolled to face him and pulled him into a hug. "I love you."

"Love you too," Hudson said. "I wouldn't go back to that picture, but I don't regret those years. We all had our own pain and heartache back then. Still do. And we all have our own healing to do, in our own ways."

I pressed a kiss to his jaw.

"Thank you," Hudson murmured.

"For what?"

"For showing me what real love is," he said, his words thick. "I was so busy convincing myself I couldn't love, couldn't be in a healthy, real relationship, I almost missed out on the love of a lifetime. Something changed the moment you walked into that coffee shop—something that was meant to grow and flourish on the foundation we started all those years ago."

I held him tight. The soft summer breeze stirring the peach trees, the heat of the day slowly giving up, and the scent of grass teasing our senses. "Never really believed the saying 'Home is where your heart is', but now I do."

"Haven Grove is the only place I'd ever want to call home."

"No," I said, my chest tight with the overflowing love I had for this man. "I mean, yes, Haven Grove is great. But I meant my true home. My heart is with you. Wherever you are, that's where my heart will be. Always."

Hudson's eyes shone in the moonlight. When he spoke, his words were heavy with emotion. "Then it's a good thing I plan on spending the rest of my life right here loving you."

~The End~

The Men of Haven Grove continues with Henry's story.
In the meantime, if you want more addictive, sexy, emotional M/M romance, check out A.D. Ellis's backlist at Amazon.
Many titles are on KindleUnlimited while several are available on all book sale platforms.

Read on for more from A.D. Ellis.

Also by A.D. ELLIS

On Cravenwood Block- the complete four-book series in a box set. Or start with Jett & Leighton in book 1 HERE.

Adore (Remington Place 1) is a steamy, age-gap, bi-awakening, dad's best friend M/M romance with a sassy smartass and a sexy silver fox. It's the first book in the Remington Place series and can be read as a stand-alone.

Crave (Remington Place 2) is a steamy, friends-to-lovers, fake relationship M/M romance with a virgin nursing student and a gruff, grumbly construction worker.

Desire (Remington Place 3) is a steamy, age-gap, hurt/comfort M/M romance featuring a heart-of-gold mechanic and a twink who's a lot stronger than he realizes. *Please note: This story has mention of sex trafficking and sexual abuse.*

Yearn (Remington Place 4)- a steamy, enemies-to-lovers, forced proximity M/M romance between two EMS workers who have hated each other for a decade.

Silver in the City (3 books- meet the Silver crew you read about in Forged in the City) Available on AUDIO!

Forged in the City (3 books- a spin-off series from Silver in the City) Available on AUDIO

Find other books here - https://books2read.com/ap/RWrrNx/AD-Ellis

About the Author

A.D. Ellis is an Indiana girl, born and raised. She spends much of her time in central Indiana as an instructional coach/teacher in the inner city of Indianapolis, being a mom to two amazing teenagers, and wondering how she and her husband of over two decades haven't driven each other insane yet. A lot of her time is also devoted to phone call avoidance and her hatred of cooking.

She loves chocolate, wine, pizza, and naps along with reading and writing romance. These loves don't leave much time for housework, much to the chagrin of her husband. Who would pick cleaning the house over a nap or a good book? She uses any extra time to increase her fluency in sarcasm.

A.D. uses she/they pronouns.

Sign up at http://www.subscribepage.com/ADEllisNewsMMRomance for a FREE book!

Website http://adellisauthor.com/

Find me EVERYWHERE at https://www.adellisauthor.com/mylinks/

Connect with A.D. Ellis

Follow my website http://www.adellisauthor.com or find me on Facebook

http://www.facebook.com/adellisauthor

If you want to get updates about releases, interviews, sales, giveaways, and more please sign up for my newsletter http://www.subscribepage.com/ADEllisNewsMMRomance

Check out my TikTok- https://www.tiktok.com/@adellisauthor

Find me on Spotify if you'd like to listen to the playlist for this book (mainly just the songs I listened to while writing). Just search for A.D. Ellis.

To make it easy, find me EVERYWHERE here- https://www.adellisauthor.com/mylinks/

Acknowledgments

It's always so hard to write this part because I'm worried I'll forget someone without meaning to.

I lost my notes (doh!) but I'm pretty sure Laura H. is responsible for the suggestion of the song "I Knew I Loved You" by Savage Garden for Hudson and Lance to dance to in the orchard.

Readers- you are the reason I write. As long as you continue reading my stories, I'll continue writing them. Thank you for your support.

Bloggers & Influencers- your support, reviews, and promotion are very much appreciated. Thank you!

My author buddies- I don't know that I could keep doing this without our brainstorm sessions, laughter, road trips, meals, wine, and friendship as my support.

Thank you to my alpha readers, betas, editors, proofreaders, and ARC readers! Your eyes and input are beyond important to me.

Brett and Gage- as usual, I doubt you even grasp how much your support, input, and friendship mean to me. This author journey has brought many wonderful things into my life, and you both are two of the BEST! I'm blessed to call you friends.

My family and friends- thank you for your love and support, always.

Cover Photo by Eric McKinney at 6:12 Photography

Cover Model: Caden J.

www.ingramcontent.com/pod-product-compliance
Lightning Source LLC
Chambersburg PA
CBHW031059020726
47495CB00007B/1961